Heaven Above, Earth Below

A Novella

By
Mark Perretta

Copyright 2016 Mark Perretta
Published by Mark Perretta
ISBN: 978-0-9971439-1-1
Cover Art copyright 2015 by Mark Perretta
Formatting and Editing Services by Wizards in
Publishing

This is a work of fiction. Names, characters,
businesses, places, events, and incidents are either
the products of the author's imagination or used in
a fictitious manner. Any resemblance to actual
persons or actual events is purely coincidental,
except for the character of Jason Mann.

~A Note from the Author~

When my career as a teacher began at Canton Central Catholic High School, little did I realize the impact my students would have on my life. I went into the profession thinking just the opposite; they were the ones that needed me. But I quickly realized, to make a difference in the world and the lives I touched, I had to acquire something more. As it turned out, my students would provide the profound ingredients needed for shaping the teacher and, ultimately, the person I would become.

When I first met Jason in 1992, I certainly had no comprehension of the impact he would make on my life or that his story would stay with me...until now.

An intelligent, good-looking young man with so much potential before him, Jason served as a member of the National Honor Society, president of his class for three years, president of Student Council his senior year, and was a member of the football, basketball, and track teams—the kind of student who made me think, "I hope if I have a son, he turns out like Jason."

I first met his parents at a "Feed the Team" event for the football team. Feed the Team is a night dedicated to players, their families, and coaches. Once a week, dinner is shared the night before a game. Later that school year, as an assistant track coach, I watched Jason participate in the 4 x 400. With him as the lead leg, the relay team won the state championship, and did so in record time.

He would go on to graduate from Duke, attending on a Navy ROTC scholarship. A four-year letter winner in Track and Field while there, he then headed to the Navy, handpicked by the Commanding Officer of VS-38 to go to the Viking Advanced Tactics and Weapons School. Top Gun for the Viking community, Jason personally flew fifty combat missions over Iraq during Operations SOUTHERN WATCH and IRAQI FREEDOM. Jason's call name was "Catdog," and he completed two deployments onboard the USS *Constellation*.

As I formulated a plan for unfolding his story, I recalled my fascination as a boy with World War II and, specifically, the tragic events of the USS *Indianapolis*. I read many stories dealing with World War II, but the ones concerning the *Indianapolis* always remained with me. Various "ideas" bounced in my head quite a few years. Then, after some fortuitous inspiration that occurred during a family vacation, I felt ready to write.

This story is fiction, but, at the same time, many items are not. I tried to be true to Jason's story. I did not want to overly conceal his identity, which is why "his" character in the story is of the same name. The fact that I used the last name Mann is symbolic and purposeful. I created many similarities of my character to the real-life Jason. Many of the details will be obvious to his family and the people who knew him, many will not.

Jason's story is meant to honor veterans everywhere, and one that can be retold, albeit with a multitude of names. My heart goes out to all families of military men and women and the sacrifices both continually make. It is because of those who serve their country with discipline, duty, and honor that enables *us* to live the lives we want.

To put your life on the line for brothers and sisters, for people you will never know, to pay the ultimate price for your country? Understanding the hearts of heroes is not an easy thing. I hope I have captured a piece of them within these pages.

Mark Perretta
Canton, Ohio
May 2016

Acknowledgements

I want to thank Lieutenant Colonel Christopher J. Francis of the United States Air Force and Lieutenant Commander Michael L. McGlynn of the United States Navy as sources for accuracy regarding technical information and advice given for the various military scenes. Thank you, Chris and O.J., for your patience, knowledge, and sacrifice.

Also, a very special thank you to Steve Dallas who took my words and made them into the song I could only imagine.

I would like to thank my dear friend Laura Adante, who encouraged me throughout the entire process and provided me with key "logic alerts" and suggestions that were vital to the story. Your knowledge, expertise, and insights are invaluable.

Finally, I would like to thank my wizard of editing, Valerie Mann. The devil is in the details, and you were the angel that rescued me.

Dedication

To Griffith

Heaven Above, Earth Below

When the world appears empty and hope is lost
And finding yourself comes at too great a cost,
No need to shut out, no need for a sign—
Fill your heart with love and open your eyes.
Often too close to perceive the truth,
Arise four simple words to heal and soothe—
Heaven above, Earth below.

When tragedy strikes and hate is abound,
Miracles happen where love can be found.
He determines every need—
Open your heart, set yourself free.
The harmony of order always restores,
And peace shall reign for evermore.
Faith provides what we already know—
Heaven above, Earth below.

Never alone in our time of strife,
The footsteps are one in our path of life.
Easy to forget, so mortal to do,
Eternal presence and life anew.
Often too close to perceive the truth,
Arise four simple words to heal and soothe—
Heaven above, Earth below.

Chapter One

Boys in Life Jackets

July 31, 1945

Somewhere in the Philippine Sea

The ocean has a way of claiming, if only by the smallest degree. And with each passing wave, something indeed was being taken. For the surviving men of the USS *Indianapolis*, hope eroded their souls.

Their mighty ship had been the length of two football fields laid end to end. Something that size is not supposed to sink in less than twelve minutes, but the impact of two enemy torpedoes broke her; she rolled and went down. Of the 1,196 men aboard, some 900, disoriented and panicky, made it into the water and soon littered the sea.

Heaven above, water below, and I am somewhere in between. The single thought became the young sailor's refrain as he bobbed in the darkness. The phrase's simple repetition grew as monotonous as the ocean itself, and, though it kept his mind occupied, he never eased thinking it. Fortunately, due to the secrecy of their mission, the men had no comprehension of the ordeal that lay ahead.

Propelled by the current's discretion, some of the sailors floated on cargo nets, others wore life jackets, and few had rafts. The truly unlucky could only swim...and wait. For when they'd hit the water, so had the scent of blood and death. It would not be long before the shark attacks began.

As they floated in darkness, whispers of prayer and quiet discussion of food and home could be heard between moans of pain. The faces of everyone were covered with the thick oil that had once powered their ship. They'd applied it to keep the sun's powerful rays from burning their faces come daylight, succeeding in giving every man a ghastly and dirty appearance.

On the first night, the surviving men eagerly awaited the warmth of the morning sun. The second and third night brought the realization that the coolness of morning would give way to scorching heat, and there would be no escape. By the forth night, they knew the next sunrise would indeed be their last.

Occasionally, rants of the dehydrated intermingled with the thrashing of human and shark in the water. The young sailor bobbed in the black ocean, its darkness filling his mind with a dismal thought—if he or any of his brothers disappeared, would anyone really know? Or better yet...care? "Heaven above, water below," he muttered. "And I am somewhere in between."

Driven by a deep sense of duty, he'd joined the Navy at eighteen. Duty led him to what he knew with certainty. He and his brothers formed the most meager-looking group of men to ever float in the ocean.

Several sailors at the front of the line hypnotically repeated the Lord's Prayer.

"Our Father, who art in heaven, hallowed be Thy name...."

Someone behind him wept in hysteria.

Another sailor cried, "Water, water everywhere." His parched throat produced the semblance of a voice, barely audible, and yet it mustered enough strength to give way to a kind of mad laughter heard by all.

Someone tried to rally spirits as darkness gave way to morning light.

"Just stay together, boys, and we will get through this!"

And without warning, the sun burst over the horizon, revealing the true color of the young man's eyes. In an ironic coincidence, his icy blues matched the ocean that engulfed him.

Everyone shielded his face as the sudden immersion into light filled their souls and gave them a renewed sense of hope.

It did not last.

"Hey! Where's Murph? Anyone seen Murph? Murphy? Murphy!"

And then someone saw it.

"Oh God! No, No!"

The shadows had returned.

"Oh shit! Here they come! Everyone stay together!"

The thrashing of water ensued, and screams and chaos quickly followed. But this time differed for the young sailor. This time he drifted, almost indifferent to his plight, no longer crying out, splashing, or making noise to scare away the shadows.

Instead of minding the water and what lurked below as he floated in the middle of some chaotic tempest of death, he gazed to the sky and caught a glimpse of an object on the horizon. It soundlessly approached, gracefully and almost unnoticed, soaring toward the men as the treachery continued below.

And when the bird flew directly overhead, he heard it—not the sound of man or ocean or beast, but rather, a quiet and soft and peaceful cadence, like the steady rain of a passing storm. Strangely, to him it seemed like musical notes descending from heaven.

But that could not be the case, and his imagination owned the better part of him. As quickly as the notes hung in the air and filled his ears, they faded. He shook his head and tried to regain his wits.

Numb, he stared as the bird disappeared into the vastness beyond. "Heaven above, water below," he whispered. "And I am somewhere in between."

Present Day

The eyes of an old man suddenly shot open, and a sound, more like a gasp than a scream, erupted from his throat. His eyes were an icy-blue color, like that of the ocean. The violent gesticulations that had gripped his body moments before eased...just another nightmare.

He found it easier not to rest any more this night. Filled with distress, he pushed upright, slipped his feet into his slippers, and moved to a nearby desk.

Clicking on the desk light, he glanced down at a half-completed structure that sat before him.

He tried not to focus on the ticking wall clock and, instead, continued the labor of building another birdhouse.

Chapter Two

Straight Lines

The Thanksgiving decorations at Michael D's reminded everyone it was getting late in the year, a fact easily lost in the warm Pensacola sun. The crowded pub danced with activity, even for a Monday night. People, trying to get served at the bar, shoved on tiptoe. The ever-present aroma of beer and pizza filled the air as exuberant conversation echoed.

John Mann sat at the bar, his youthful good looks betraying the fact he could legally drink. He grabbed two shot glasses filled with whiskey. Taking the first, he handed it to his best friend, and then, without hesitation, raised the second and proposed a toast.

"The word of the day is legs," he said. "Let's

spread the word."

A muffled laugh escaped his friend, who raised his glass in salute. The whiskey went down in one, quick gulp.

Their friendship had formed at a young age; they had grown up in neighboring homes. But their similarities ended there. Where John had light-brown hair and blue eyes, Steve had dark hair and dark eyes. John was vocal and daring, tall and athletic. Steve was quiet and reserved, short and non-athletic. Together, they were the most perfect foil a friendship ever knew.

Megan, a hint of disdain curling her lips, watched their antics. She'd first met John, the cute one with the corny jokes, a little over a year earlier. She whispered into his ear, "John, it's getting late. Tomorrow is an important day for you."

"Megan, relax. Try and enjoy yourself." The ever-present smile fixed on his tanned face urged her to calm. "Tomorrow can wait."

"So, you've thought about tomorrow?" Steve blurted.

"Thanks. I'm trying not to."

She slammed her bottle on the counter, the contents splashing his shirt. "Jesus, John! You'd better start thinking about it. What time do you have to be there anyway?"

He brushed the liquid from his sleeve. "Hammer Time?"

Steve raised his hand quickly to his lips, trying to catch the laugh before it escaped, but the alcohol had started to take effect and his reflexes were slowing.

"Daytime?"

She spun away, anger flashing in her eyes, and, for a moment, John thought he'd gone too far. Catching her by the wrist, he tried to pull her into his arms. She planted her hand on his chest to keep him at arm's length.

"You know I can't help myself." His head dropped in disappointment. "You're not mad at me, are you? Meg, I'm...."

Playing the role of indifference, she refused to acknowledge him.

"Meg, look at me! One more drink and then we'll head out. I promise."

"You're being an ass."

"But you still love me...right?"

"Honestly? I'm not quite sure right now."

He gave her a peck on the cheek and then

released her.

Steve tried to change the subject. "How's work?"

John winced. "Thanks, Steve. You're on a roll." Turning back to Megan, he searched for the right words. "I know...I didn't tell you...yet, but...."

Her mouth contorted, and her disappointment rose. "What'd you do now?"

"I just didn't see myself making a career out of waiting on tables, so...."

"So?"

"So, let's just say I am searching for employment again."

"Damn it, John! How could you quit? That's your second job in three months. You need the money!"

He'd arrived at the end of her patience, and, lowering his gaze at her disappointed tone, he spoke as if admonishing his shoes. "The place was driving me insane. It's a mindless job!" He met her eyes before continuing. "The manager was always asking me to wear buttons, having to parade around the restaurant with the right amount of 'flair,' and the tables...."

"What about 'em?" Steve gulped the rest of his

beer.

"Every day starts and ends with me having to adjust the lines of every tabletop so they all point in the same direction. Who cares what direction they're pointing? Besides, a man with my kind of talent?"

Speechless, Megan had heard enough and burned a stare through him.

"I can find something much better." He almost believed himself when he added, "Trust me. I know what I'm doing."

"Famous last words." Steve's mutter dripped with sarcasm.

Through clenched teeth, she continued, "Like you knew what you were doing when you said you were defending my honor?"

John recoiled from her outburst. "Okay, okay, so that was a little extreme."

"I could've taken care of myself!"

"But, Meg, the guy deserved it! Didn't he?" He paused. "Didn't he? I was just trying to protect you." Grasping her hand, he placed her fingers to his lips and kissed them with the tenderness that had first made her melt.

"I-I guess," she relented. "But you still have to

explain it to the judge tomorrow. And if we don't leave now, you can forget about this weekend."

Steve leaned on the bar top with both elbows. "What's this weekend?"

John motioned to the bartender. "Check, please!" He smirked at his friend. "Don't you worry about it."

Chapter Three

Lessons of Service

The general chaos of John's room belied the fact he'd grown up the son of a military man. Though discipline, order, and responsibility were the rails of his family, the train had been thrown off track since his father's death. Carolyn, John's mother, tried not to be too demanding on her children because of that early tragedy. And that worked fine with John's brother Jason.

But as parents can attest, raising different children in the same family does not guarantee the same results, or, for that matter, even similar results. Where Jason had been her rock and served as a 29-year-old lieutenant in the Navy, his brother remained a constant worry.

Time had worn seriousness into her look and

demeanor, but despite her forty-nine years, she was still attractive. Her light-brown hair had given way to more than a hint of gray. That was the least of her concerns.

Typically, she spent her day as a legal secretary. But today seemed different, and that different was not a good different.

"John! You up?"

She flung his bedroom door open, and it slammed against the doorstop. "You're going to be late!" Throwing the lights on, she decided to attack the curtains before targeting her wrath toward her son. "Get your butt up! We have to be there in forty-five minutes!"

An unintelligible groan emanated from the bed as the morning sunlight poured through the window. "I need a drink," he croaked. Carolyn stopped in her tracks. "Of water."

"Maybe you shouldn't stay out so damned late! And *maybe* you should set your alarm a little earlier! Get dressed, we have to go."

He rolled onto his back, spread his arms to each side of the mattress, and stared at the ceiling. When the sudden, shrill sound of the alarm broke through, he grabbed a pillow to cover his head, and, just as suddenly, she ripped it away.

"Move it!"

Crawling from his bed, he silenced the buzzer, knowing just as his mother did, this indeed would not be a good day.

***

John sat next to his mother. His nine-year-old sister, Jennifer, relaxed in the backseat, reading Marvel's *The Peril and the Power*, starring The Fantastic Four. He glanced back, saw the comic's cover, and thought about the peril he faced and the fact he had little power to stop what was about to occur.

The drive to the courthouse lasted less than fifteen minutes, but that morning he wished it had taken fifteen days. Though his first time in a courtroom, he knew deep down he probably should have been there on a couple of other occasions. Luckily, his mother never knew.

The Mann family pulled into the parking lot, and, for the first time, John noticed the piercing sunlight. Six evenly set Doric columns greeted visitors at the entrance of the Pensacola County

Courthouse. As they entered the building and passed through security, Carolyn's lawyer met them. From there, they ushered themselves into a conference room and then to the courtroom itself.

Luckily for John, it was a pre-trial conference and his lawyer had already worked out the details. They stood as the judge entered the courtroom and lowered himself onto the wood chair behind the bench.

"John Mann." He opened a folder and hesitated. "Your father...Roy? Brother is Jason?"

Sheepish, John nodded and settled beside his lawyer.

The judge rubbed his chin with his left hand and reminisced with fondness. "Roy and I went to grade school together. And your brother? The best high school miler I've ever seen. My son ran track at Central. Always had a smile on his face. How is he doing these days?"

"He's doing well, sir. He flies fighter jets in the Navy."

The judge straightened his glasses and any semblance of a smile disappeared. He interlocked his fingers and rested one clenched fist on the desk, the change in his temperament palpable to John.

"Mr. Mann, your behavior is, shall I say, less than desirable. Your actions were reckless. It is time for you to grow up. Responsibility. Accountability. But most of all, you need to learn to be a man of honor. I know this is something your family is quite familiar with. Control yourself and your actions, even if *you* think you have just cause."

He scribbled some notes into a folder and handed them to a clerk before returning his full attention to John. "Your lawyer, on behalf of your mother, has also expressed trepidation about your behavior in general. Sometimes, when we're growing up, we're more concerned with acquiring, not inspiring, with getting, not giving."

Despite his anxiety, John met the man's gaze.

"John, do you know who Arthur Ashe was?"

"No, sir."

"Mr. Ashe was one of the finest professional tennis players the US ever had, but at the same time, so much more. His commitment to social justice, health, and people in general helped change the world. He once said, 'Life is not the urge to surpass others at whatever cost, but the urge to serve others at whatever cost.' That's what is heroic, not defending through reckless behavior. Due to the fact you have no priors, and since your lawyer has submitted a guilty plea, I am sentencing you to 250 hours of community service at St. Francis Assisted Living. You need to learn to serve others before yourself."

The gavel struck the sound block, and the noise reverberated through John's being.

"Stay out of trouble, son."

Without a word and visibly disappointed, John lowered his gaze and drew a deep breath. The Manns stepped into the anteroom, where he stood next to his pig-tailed sister, still clutching her comic book. Carolyn managed a smile for John's attorney, spoke a few quiet words, and shook his hand before spinning toward the exit. Her children fell in line.

As they passed security and back through the pillars, a dazzling brightness engulfed them. Despite the day's proceedings inside, all seemed right outside.

They slipped into their car, and Carolyn placed the key to the ignition but stopped, staring straight ahead at nothing in particular. Before John could speak, his mother broke the silence. "You can't do this to me anymore." She sounded exhausted. "I can't do this anymore."

Opening his mouth for a reply, he reconsidered. *No, this is definitely not the time.*

She started the engine and headed for home. He leaned his head against the window, its cool glass refreshing on the side of his warm face.

Jennifer's attention switched to another comic. "Mommy, what is a miler?"

"Why do you ask, honey?"

"The judge said Jason was the best miler he's ever seen."

A faint smile came to her mother's lips. "It means that he was a very good runner. A miler is someone who runs a mile...four laps around a track. Like the judge said, Jason became one of the best. His last lap is what separated him from others."

"Why is that?"

Carolyn wet her lips and glanced at John. "It means he knew how to finish what he started and do it with determination and discipline."

"Is that where all of those medals came from?"

"Yes, dear."

"I'm going to be a miler someday, too, Mommy."

John looked over his shoulder and squinted at his sister.

"You just do the best at whatever you try, honey," their mother said. "That's what's important."

***

She pulled into the driveway, hit the brakes with more force than necessary, and put the car in park. "I'm late for work. There are leftovers in the fridge for lunch. I'll see you tonight."

Brother and sister stepped out of the car and headed for the house. Carolyn put the car in reverse, began to pull away, and then rolled down the window. "John, take care of your sister."

He nodded.

"'Bye, Mommy! Love you!" Jennifer yelled.

"Love you," Carolyn replied. Her stern countenance gave way to a hint of a smile. "Both!" She gave her son a wink and put the car in gear again.

As she pulled away, she caught a glimpse of John in the rearview mirror. Once again, he reminded her so much of Roy.

Chapter Four

Catdog

The single-piece canopy of an F-18 Hornet provides its pilots with an exceptional 360-degree view. For Jason Mann his favorite feature of the jet delivered him one of the great ironies of flying. Sitting in such a small cockpit, he frequently marveled at the canopy above and how it opened to the world below. Almost like a God's-eye view of a universe, it belonged only to him.

Heaven above, Earth below….

The words rang in his mind as he sat snugly in the cockpit of his powerful jet.

"And I am somewhere in between," he muttered. The bulky headgear concealed his sandy-blond hair and bright-blue eyes. Radio chatter filled his helmet one second but ended abruptly the next.

The quick switch to silence snapped Jason's thoughts to the single best moment in his life, the time he proposed to his wife.

He'd gone for a jog with Sarah and her golden retriever, Gypsy, at a park. Purchasing the ring several weeks earlier, he'd wanted to wait until a romantic trip to Paris. But an afternoon run changed his mind; he could wait no longer.

He ran awkwardly, the leash in one hand, the ring in his pocket. He checked and double-checked every few hundred yards to make sure it had not fallen out. Beads of sweat gathered on his forehead—and not from the exertion of running.

Overcome with nerves, he jerked to a sudden halt, spun, and fell on one knee.

Sarah's long dark hair, wrapped in a ponytail, continued to bounce until she slowed and turned curiously. "What?" She came to a full stop.

He swallowed then tried to wet his lips, his tongue as useful as a piece of sandpaper.

Voice rising, she asked again, "What? You hurt? Are you sick? Did you pull a muscle again?" She stepped toward him.

"I think I did pull something." His voice quavered as he reached into his pocket. "It's not what I planned, but I can't wait any longer. Will you marry me?"

Her mouth fell open, and her eyes shimmered like the diamond in his hand. "Oh, Jason!" She jumped into his arms and knocked him over.

"Is that a yes?" He laughed underneath, still clutching the ring.

She pinned him to the ground and tears began to roll. "Yes, yes...of course, of course!"

Gypsy joined the celebration and gave his face an approving lick.

"Sarah," he said.

"What?"

"I think when you tackled me...I really did pull something."

Suddenly, the COM crackled to life, and he snapped out of his flashback.

"Catdog 3, Contact BRAA 350, 8, 15 thousand."

"CatDog 3, visual," he replied.

"Catdog 3, roger."

"In one-point-five mile trail. Contact descending."

Jason flicked his standard stick controller, and the F-18 banked to the right in a blink and disappeared into the clouds.

Chapter Five

A Little Off

The table in the Mann household always held a place for family. Whether during the meals they ate, the stories they told, or the homework for school, the important thing was being together. Everyone would share and be content. Roy asked each child at dinner what happened at school that day. A detailed report of every class followed.

And if one of his children ever responded with the eyebrow-raising *nothing*, after the dreaded "What did you do at school today?", that child would have to handwrite a two-page report specifying the *nothing*. Carolyn insisted on keeping the tradition alive, but that evening the ritual was lost.

Jennifer took the lull in conversation as an

opportunity to sneak her Batman comic book to the table.

"Jennifer, what have I told you about reading at the table while we eat?" Carolyn asked. "This is family time."

"Sorry, Mommy. Batman just arrested the bad guys." She shoved the comic under her chair and, without cue, began a ten-minute dissertation on her day. The monologue included a detailed analysis on the bones of the human hand, followed by a story of a hurt finger during a heated kickball game at the playground and an art project to be done with marshmallows.

When she finished, John began his recap, but an unexpected two words slipped from his mouth.

"This sucks."

"Excuse me?" Carolyn gave him a deadly warning look.

Without replying, he played with his food.

"I think the meatloaf is good, Mommy," Jennifer said, oblivious to the storm about to come.

Her mother ignored her. "John...like the judge said, it's time you grow up. I have been responsible for almost everything in this household. I need your help. I can't do it by myself any longer!"

"But a retirement home? I haven't been in something like that since Dad—"

Carolyn dropped her fork and buried her head in her hands.

"Mom, I'm sorry. I know I've been a little off lately."

"A little?" Her voice increased an octave. "For Christ's sake, John. Not only did you flatten all four of your boss's tires, you spray-painted his car!"

"We're painting in school." Jennifer smiled. "I'm painting a picture of Batman tomorrow."

He shot his sister a disgusted sideways glance. "Mom, I know the guy is...*was* my boss and all, but he was beyond drunk and being an ass—"

She struck her son with a glare that stopped him mid-word. He covered Jennifer's ears and mouthed the word with vehemence.

Pulling his hands back, he finished his sentence. "To Megan. I promise to turn it around. I just don't think it's fair that I have to spend 250 hours in a retirement home of all things."

"Maybe he was hard on you to try and teach you a lesson. Anyway, you're lucky he didn't give you something more permanent! Jason would have never—"

"I know, I know. Jason would have never done anything like this. I'm just not as—"

Carolyn pounded her fists on the dining room table. The plates jumped to attention, and Jennifer stared at her, round-eyed.

"I'm sorry, but this is not about Jason! This is about you!"

Unable to continue the argument, she broke off, rolled her head back and exhaled, not knowing what to say.

"Mommy?" Jennifer whispered.

She closed her eyes. "What?"

"Asshole is a bad word, isn't it?"

Her head fell into her hands once again, and a smile formed on John's face. He concealed it with a napkin before she noticed.

Carolyn pulled her short fingers away from her face. "Jennifer, John said something he shouldn't have. Please don't ever say that again."

"Sorry, Mommy." She stuck her tongue out at her brother, who returned the favor.

Searching for the right words, their mother continued, "Megan told me you quit your job again. What are you going to do for money?"

He sat in silence and shrugged.

27

Finally, the dam broke.

"You need to wake the hell up!" She pointed at him. "You're the man of the house, and it's time you started acting like it!"

"Now, you *sound* like him," John muttered.

"Your father would—"

He finished her sentence hollowly. "Be disappointed?"

"More like heartbroken."

The family sat motionless at the table. Jennifer lifted her fork, twirling and fixating on it. Carolyn rolled her head to the side, not knowing what to say. An awkward silence descended on the table.

"I'm sorry, Mom. I didn't mean to—"

"Just help me clean the table and pack Jennifer's lunch for tomorrow." She pushed the back of her legs against the chair and stood. The chair screeched on the wooden floor. Grabbing some dishes, she disappeared into the kitchen.

Jennifer gave her brother a questioning look. Knowing he'd gone too far, he winked to try and make her smile.

"Let's help." They cleared the rest of the table.

As they walked into the kitchen and placed the dishes next to the sink, Carolyn turned to Jennifer.

"It's after eight. Time for bed, honey."

"Okay, Mommy."

"And don't forget to brush your teeth."

"I won't."

"And give me a kiss." Carolyn knelt.

Jennifer threw her arms around her mother's neck and kissed her on the cheek. With that, she spun and left the room. Carolyn focused her frustration on the dishes and began to scrub.

Packing his sister's lunch, John grabbed her favorite spread, strawberry jelly, from the refrigerator, and then had an idea. He pulled a piece of paper and a pen out of a drawer and scribbled, *Dear Jennifer, Don't forget to eat your carrots. Carrots help my x-ray vision! Love, Superman.*

As he placed the note between a bag of carrots and a napkin, the thought of his sister reading it the next day brought a smile to his face. He closed her Spider-Man lunch box and put it into the refrigerator. But his grin erased as he remembered the morning in court and what lay ahead for him.

"Mom," he said. "I'll go tomorrow after class. I promise."

His mother simply nodded and continued to

work. There was nothing left to say—he had to show her. He walked out of the kitchen and toward his bedroom.

At the sink, Carolyn drew a deep breath and stopped her work. She set the dish gently down and made her way to the family room. One of the walls was covered with photographs. Some of the pictures were color, some black and white, but all of family.

A framed photograph of Carolyn, Roy, Jason, John and Jennifer hanging on the wall caught her attention. *Jennifer's just an infant.* Staring at the picture, Carolyn lost herself. She reached to touch it as faint voices of her children in the neighboring room crept into her ears.

"So is your homework done?" John said.

"What do you think?" Jennifer answered.

"When's the last time you cleaned your room?"

"Like you should talk."

Their mother touched a few of the surrounding photographs as if they needed adjusting. Roy, posing in military dress, stared back at her from one of them.

Her attention traveled to the center of the wall,

where a framed medal of honor from Roy's service days hung at the heart of the collage. She drew a breath, managed a warm thought and half a smile.

John's voice echoed down the hallway. "So, what's the deal with Batman? Is he a bat or a man?"

Chapter Six

Supergirl

"C'mon, Jenn. We gotta go. It's time for school."

John knocked on Jennifer's locked bedroom door. A pink poster stating "Girls Rule" stared back at him. Still no answer came from within. This time he beat the door, his knuckles signaling an urgent appeal. Finally, a reply echoed from inside.

"What's the secret password?"

He rolled his eyes. "The secret pass...?" Suddenly, he remembered her weakness for kryptonite.

"Fortress of solitude!"

The door opened from the inside with one swift movement, and Jennifer stood ready for school.

He quickly muttered, "Let's go!" and headed

down the hallway. "I'm gonna be late!"

***

During the brief drive to Jennifer's school, it seemed to be one of those days. John hit every traffic light known to automobiles. His timeframe increased along with his impatience. He didn't want to be late to class...again.

She read her comic in the backseat. "Is Superman a hero?"

The question surprised John. "Of course he is."

"Why?"

"Well, Superman is brave. He can't be defeated, and he fights for justice. He defends those who can't defend themselves, and he wears a very cool cape."

"Do you know any heroes?"

"Do I know any heroes?" He grasped for an answer and scratched his head. "Of course I do." Pulling into the school parking lot, he stopped the car.

"Are there more heroes or villains in the world?"

John twisted toward his sister, his eyes sending

her a silent appeal to hurry, and waited for her to get out of the vehicle. She sat there waiting for an answer before trying her brother again, louder than before. "*Are* there more heroes or villains?"

"Umm...heroes."

"Are you sure?" She fidgeted with her comic and book bag.

"Yes, of course. Jen, come on! I'm gonna be late for class."

He hurried out of the car and opened the passenger door for her. She put the comic in her backpack, careful not to bend a page, and stepped out.

"Easy pateasy, okay, okay! See ya tonight."

John slammed the door closed as Jennifer headed toward the entrance of the school. He made his way back around the car and, just before he jumped in, glanced at his sister. "See ya tonight...."

She spun toward her brother.

"Supergirl!"

A smile beamed on her face as John drove away.

***

Pensacola Community College was a crowded campus when John arrived. Many students hurried to class, some lounged and talked, while others played with their cell phones and laptop computers.

Making his way to the philosophy wing of the science center, he passed through a crowded hallway into the class and took his place in the hundred-seat lecture room.

Dr. Carol Shelly taught the class, and though she had a diminutive 5'2" stature, she considered her ideas quite grandiose. Her voice frequently boomed rants of wisdom. Today would be no different.

Hurrying, John sat between Megan and Steve, removed his backpack, and reached for his notebook. "Sup!"

"Sup," Steve said.

John winked at Megan. "Hey, babe."

At the front of the room, Shelly thrust the class into a lecture on truth, justice, and the philosophical way.

Megan whispered into his ear, "Please tell me you're going to begin today. You *need* to go."

"I know. I will, just don't worry."

"Then don't give me a reason to!"

He squeezed her hand.

In the front of the room, Shelly hammered away. Her preachy, righteous style always gave him the indication she alone seemed to know the definition of truth.

She stood behind the podium, her voice dominant. "Understand that living a life with truth, honor, and integrity means taking a stand for what you know is right no matter the consequences. If you do, others will follow."

Chapter Seven

Finding His Way

The motto at Saint Francis Assisted Living Community hung for all to see upon entering the handsome building. It also proved to be sadly ironic. A large banner declared, *Kick off the good life!* Unfortunately, for many residents the good life had already kicked off, four quarters had been played, and all that remained...sudden death.

John sauntered through the large white front doors and into the well-lit atrium of the building. A nurses' station sat in the middle of an open area with two nurses behind a marble counter. One typed on a computer while the other put aside her paperwork and smiled as he approached.

"May I help you?"

"I'm John Mann. I am here to.... Is there a

nurse named Nancy here?"

"Nancy? Yes. Have a seat and I'll page her for you."

He moved to the side of the station and settled on an ornate red-cushioned chair that seemed like it belonged in some important library. He didn't know why that particular chair sat there because it appeared, even to him, out of place. He also didn't know why a particular memory entered his mind, but the last time he'd seen a similar chair, he'd been seven.

Carolyn and Roy had brought their two sons to the shopping mall to sit on Santa's lap and take some pictures. Apparently, John did nothing but cry, and Jason made a point of retelling the story every Christmas.

John leaned his head back and chuckled.

His gaze lifted toward the huge circular clock hanging in front of him. The ebony hands marked the time: 3:26 p.m. The walls of the atrium were rather plain, other than the numerous plants streaming from various levels. They added color, but all screamed artificial.

A kind voice emerged from behind. "John? John Mann?"

He rose and turned, reaching for the open hand extended toward him.

"I'm Nurse Nancy," she said. "I am the head nurse here at Saint Francis."

Nurse Nancy had a cherubic bearing. A plump woman of about forty years, she had the combination of kind face and kind voice that had to be comforting to the numerous residents, or at least the families that checked them into the building.

"Nice to meet you." The thought of another 249 hours and 59 minutes of "community service" began to sink into his mind.

"These are for you." She handed him a green T-shirt proudly displaying in bold, white letters, *St. Francis Assisted Living* across the front, along with a badge on a white lanyard that read *STAFF*.

"When you arrive, make sure you check in at the nurses' station. You need to keep an accurate time log of your hours spent here for court records."

He exhaled and stared at the floor before raising his eyes. "What do I have to do?"

"It varies. Today, I want you to make yourself familiar with the building and the residents."

"You want me to just walk around?"

"I want you to meet some of the residents. Be

friendly. Make them feel like they're someone special."

He pulled the T-shirt over his head in one quick movement that hid the disgusted look on his face for just a second. Lanyard in hand, he moved down the hall.

"And, John...."

He slowed to a stop and spun lazily.

"Make them feel important, like you'd want to be treated."

He nodded and flashed a grin for effect. "I will."

"And don't forget the lanyard." Nurse Nancy motioned to put it on and smiled. Heading to the right, she disappeared down a corridor.

He hung the badge around his neck and strode through the doors that led to the residents' living area.

The hallway flowed into a center community room. It had a color television, some cheap artwork on the walls, and a pale-blue carpet with green toggles.

Some of the residents chatted at a nearby table and sipped coffee and tea. Two more played chess. Another wore a cowboy hat while watching a baseball game on the television. An ignored piano sat in the corner of the room. John moved through the community room and into the living area. Along the way, retirees hobbled by, aided with an assortment of canes and walkers.

He forced a couple of smiles and a head nod until he passed one particular resident in a wheelchair. The timeworn woman appeared to be over eighty and eyed John. After what seemed longer than an average glare should take, he became unnerved.

Finally, he spoke. "What?"

She continued to eye him.

"What?" he asked again, a little louder.

"You work here?"

"No, just visiting."

"Then why are you wearing a badge that says 'staff'?"

"Do you *need* something?"

"I *need* to use the facilities."

"Don't you know where they're at?"

"I *need*...to *use*...the facilities!" Her shrill voice rose.

"Okay, Okay." He spun for help. "I'll get someone. Wait here."

He left her and did not turn back. Continuing through the hallway, he passed a room where an elderly woman rested on her bed, staring at a wall. Frank Sinatra's crooning echoed from within. He moved on, passed another room or two, but nothing seemed to stand out.

This is going to be the most miserable 250 hours of my life.

Finally, he stopped. "That's strange."

Backing up and peering inside, he noticed an undecorated room except for one odd detail; at least two dozen birdhouses were lined and stacked along the floor and walls. The room had one desk light at a worktable where another birdhouse sat, half completed. Immediately, his interest caught the best of him and he entered the room.

The space appeared empty except for some wooden lighthouses on a dresser and shelf. A stack of very old newspapers sat on a nearby desk next to an unmade bed. He picked up the top one, a yellowed paper dated 1945. Dropping it on the pile, he noticed a framed medal partially concealed underneath. The wooden frame contained a red, white, and blue ribbon attached to a bronze medal of valor. John moved the papers to better read the inscription sitting below the medal and on a small, rectangular piece of brass. *To the honorable men who served intrepidly aboard the USS Indianapolis.*

A gruff voice shattered the silence. "Who the hell are you?"

Emerging from the shadows and stepping into a pool of light was an old man. John almost fell over the desk from surprise. The man appeared to be in his early nineties, his eyes piercing-blue and, much to John's surprise, a head full of gray hair. Despite his age, it became apparent he was still knotted with muscle.

"And what makes you think you can just barge into my room?" A hearing aid dangled from his left ear.

"I...ah...I was...just...ah...."

The Old Man's weathered face reddened, and the veins in his forehead began to bulge, letting John know he perceived his behavior as brazen and unacceptable. "You what? For Christ's sake, spit it out, son."

"I was...ahh...just...." John stammered again.

The man squinted at him and continued to size him up.

Remembering Nurse Nancy and hoping not to get into trouble on his first day, John tried to ameliorate the situation. "Were you in the Navy? My brother's in the Navy."

The Old Man gawked in disbelief but didn't reply.

"How'd you get the medal? What'd you do? Did you...?"

With a snort from his nose that sounded like a bull about to charge, the man spun to his work desk and clicked on the light.

"Get wounded in battle?"

Focused on the birdhouse, he ignored John and grabbed a piece of sandpaper. His hands and arms were dotted with old-age liver spots. "Navy boy, huh?" growled the Old Man. "Son, I'm busy, so if that's all, I am going to get back to work."

"What're you doing?"

"I'm knitting a sweater. What the hell does it look like?" His delicate touch on the structure betrayed his callous demeanor. He continued to sand for some time before he paused and looked up to see John watching. He put the sandpaper down. "Don't you have something better to do?"

The Old Man impressed John. "Not really. Let's

just say I'm going to be helping out around here the next few months." His instinct led him not to let the Old Man know the real reason he'd come to St. Francis. "I walked by and I saw your birdhouses. That's when I...ahh...barged in."

"What do you mean 'helping out?' Did you get a job here?"

"Not quite."

"Then why the hell are you wearing a badge that says 'staff'? And for shit's sake, son, you're wearing a shirt that says 'Saint Francis Assisted Living'!"

Embarrassed, John confessed. "It's more like volunteering. I...ahhh...have to...ummm...complete something."

"Complete something?"

He delayed before giving in to the question. "250 hours of community service."

"What'd you do anyway? Rob a bank?"

He smiled. "Mmmm...no, not quite. I was...just trying to make myself 'more familiar' here." The last words echoed in sarcasm. "I was curious by what I saw in your room...your birdhouses."

"Yeah, you know what curiosity did to the cat?" He leaned back into his chair and exhaled as if to signal a white flag being raised. "Look, kid, I've been here six-and-a-half years. I served in the Navy during World War II."

"Did you kill Nazis? Or some Japs?"

"No, I didn't kill Nazis or Japs." The Old Man hesitated and his voice lowered. "At least not with a gun." He picked up a new piece of sandpaper and resumed smoothing the wood.

"How'd you win the medal?"

His silence made John feel even more unwelcome. The time had come to leave. "I'm really sorry about...." John stopped as he neared the door. "I'm going to be around quite a bit over the next few months. Is it okay if I stop by again?"

The Old Man growled in reply and continued to sand.

"Sorry, I didn't mean to be so.... Sorry."

John exited the room when suddenly the Old Man's voice called, "Hey, son."

John thrust his head back into the room.

"Get a haircut!"

He shot him a smirk and continued down the hallway with his head down, hoping not to have any more encounters with residents. He turned a corner, glanced up, and spotted a woman in a wheelchair, her back to him. Though he couldn't see her face, she was the one who'd needed to use the restroom. John pivoted the other direction. After three steps, he stopped and bit his lip.

Nurse Nancy's words haunted him. *And, John, treat them like you want to be treated.*

Approaching the back of the wheelchair, he pushed it. "My name is John."

Her arms shot and grabbing both armrests, she glanced back. "Great. Now get me to one or you're going to have a mess on your hands."

He pushed the wheelchair faster.

"Where'd you go anyway? Get lost?"

"Let's just say...." He searched for his next words. "I'm still finding my way."

Chapter Eight

Blue Light Special

Jason Mann sat quietly in his ten-by-ten foot room. As he examined his quarters, he chuckled at his Spartan existence. He found a great sense of irony in how confined he could feel on the enormous ship. But when he flew, nothing could contain him.

He took a mental inventory of the room's contents. Two sets of metal lockers, drawers, a fold-down desk and a bunk bed. Throw in a sink, a medicine chest, and a small television and that was it. Only slightly more *homey* than the prison cells he recalled in the movies, but to him "Connie" meant home. And while "Connie" was a strange way to refer to the USS *Constellation*, a Kitty Hawk-class super carrier and home to more than six

48

thousand men and women at any one time, it was how sailors always referred to their beloved ships—with affection.

He sat at the desk, drinking a cup of coffee and reading a newspaper from his hometown. Luckily, Sarah sent the paper along with the usual care-package items. He still liked the feel of the newspaper in his hands as opposed to reading it online like his younger comrades. He reminisced about evenings when his father sat in "his" chair, reading "his" paper in its entirety. Jason and John had known better than to bother their father during "his" time.

A knock echoed in the tiny room.

"Enter!" he yelled.

The door swung open, and his commanding officer stepped before him. Jason rose to attention and saluted.

The officer returned the gesture. "At ease." He hesitated. "Lieutenant, I have some...hmmm. How shall I put this?"

Jason became concerned. His pilot sense told him any hesitation was dangerous.

The CO searched for his next words. "I have some...." With that, he broke into a wide grin.

"Good news, very good news. You get to go home a little early. You're an early det. The squadron will be joining you three weeks from now in Pensacola."

Jason's mind raced. *I'm done. I'm leaving. My tour is over.* The thoughts of Sarah and home and his family engulfed him.

The CO glanced at a nearby dresser to a framed picture of him and Sarah on their honeymoon. "I suppose you may want to break the good news to her?" he asked, indicating the photograph.

Jason chuckled. "My wife Sarah, sir. I think you're right, sir. She may be interested. Besides, I'll need a ride home from the airport."

The officer smiled and extended his hand. "And, Jason, it has been my pleasure. You are one of the finest I have ever commanded."

With a firm grip, he shook his hand. "Thank you, sir."

The other man spun toward the door. "I won't keep you any more from sharing that news. Best of luck, son. Godspeed." And with that, he disappeared through the doorway.

Jason hesitated for a moment and gathered his thoughts. He knew what he had to do first. Darting through the narrow door and almost cracking his head on the top of the frame, he went in search of a "blue-light special."

Scattered around the ship, phones were provided for sailors to call loved ones when off duty. The blue phones were in constant use. Lines of sailors wishing to use them always varied in length as each waited their turn. Only on a very rare occasion could one find an unused sailor phone, hence the affectionate code words tagged to them, "blue-light special."

His favorite phone sat port side next to the barbershop. As he raced down the passageway, he whistled a seven-tone melody that had stuck with him the last few weeks. He didn't know where the tune came from, but it seemed a happy one and matched his mood in perfect harmony.

When he arrived, not only did Jason find a blue-light special but also a dial tone when he picked up the receiver. A good connection. It truly was his lucky day. The phones were spaced about three to four feet apart, which meant no privacy when they were used.

But on this day, he didn't care who heard the good news.

***

In Pensacola, a phone rang at the Mann household. Sarah, in the middle of painting a room, threw her paintbrush to the floor. Paint splattered across the tarp as she ran to the phone in anticipation.

"Hello?"

"Sarah? It's me, honey."

"Jason! It's about time you called! Is everything okay?" Gypsy barked her approval in the background.

"Yes, honey, everything is fine. Guess what? I have a surprise for you, a big surprise. You're not going to believe this. I get to.... Hey, how's the dog doing? How's work?"

"Jason! Quit kidding around! You know we've got to make this quick. Every minute we talk is a dollar!"

"Then we're having a five-dollar conversation with a million-dollar message. I'm coming home, baby! I'm an early det!"

"An early what?"

"An early detachment! My tour is over early. I just talked to my CO. I'm coming home! And don't call Mom. I want it to be a surprise."

"Oh thank God! Jason, I love you so much. How long will it take to get home?"

"I'm going to pack right now and board a plane. I'll call you when we're close to landing. See you soon, honey. I love you."

"Love you, too. I can't believe this! I miss you so much! Call me as soon as you can! Be safe."

He hung up the phone and paused, not sure the happiness he experienced was real or imagined. He pinched himself to confirm its reality and headed back to the stateroom to pack. A definite lightness in his stride, he flew through the corridor. His mind raced with thoughts of preparation and arrival.

And before realizing it, Jason began to whistle his seven-note melody.

***

Carolyn sat alone at the kitchen table and folded laundry as if in a meditative state. A television hummed in the background. Her day had been a busy one and seemed to blend with every day before. Wake, work, prepare dinner, do laundry, go to sleep, and start over the next morning. As she folded one of John's T-shirts, she lost herself in the moment. Roy'd had one just like it.

Of course, that couldn't be a difficult thing to imagine, for Roy had kept many T-shirts. His frugality came from his grandparents, growing up on their farm. They wasted nothing. He'd learned the virtue quite well. She chuckled recalling the constant battle to discard clothing that had become ragged from constant use.

"If you wear this one more time," she'd threatened Roy, "you will never see it again after it goes to the wash!" But somehow it always made its way back to her husband.

She gently placed the folded shirt on John's pile. On cue, he strolled into the kitchen, sat and smiled as if he needed something. She wanted to talk to him.

"Mom, I need to talk to you."

And that seemed like the perfect opportunity.

"Can you help me for a minute?" she asked.

He went to the laundry room with her and carried a basket of clothes back to the kitchen table. Grabbing another T-shirt, she started to fold once again. A raised eyebrow signaled complete surprise as he joined her.

"You realize this was the first time I have been in a retirement home since Dad died."

"I know," she said.

"As a kid, all I could remember was the smell. It was almost like the smell of death. Every time in his room, around the halls. Do you remember?"

"Of course." She paused and drew a deep breath. "There are certain memories that're just ingrained into your being. Graduating from high school, your first love, the moment your children are born, but also the not-so-pleasant ones."

"I could ignore the sounds of the machines, the hum of the air mattress, but the smell. The smell always hung in the air and it remained, staying with us even when we left."

It was the first time in a long time John had reflected about life with her in such a serious manner. She appreciated his candor and thoughtfulness. "It was a very difficult time for us all, but...yes, a smell always seemed to linger."

He licked his lips and continued, "Today wasn't like I thought it would be. It seemed...different."

"Was that a good different?"

"Yeah, it was a good different." A slow smile

crept across his face. "I met a World War II vet at St. Francis today. He was in the Navy. Won a medal for something. He makes birdhouses, of all things."

Carolyn returned the smile and grabbed another shirt to fold.

"I've been doing a lot of thinking lately and I just want to say...I'm sorry."

She stopped and placed the shirt on the pile.

"I want to make you proud. I want Dad to be proud."

"Oh, John, he would be proud. He would just want what I want, and that's for you to be the best man you can be."

"Like you said, I need to wake up."

"We all make mistakes in life. It doesn't make you a bad person, but you have to see it as an opportunity to learn, and grow, to become better."

"I know, Mom. And I want you to know that I see everything you do for me and Jennifer." He stood and kissed his mother on the cheek.

Carolyn tried not to show her surprise. Reaching out, she touched his hand with maternal tenderness. Moments like that were rare for mother and son. His demeanor and affection made it a moment to treasure.

John moved to the doorway then spun toward her again. "You know...." He hesitated. "His eyes...his eyes were the color of the ocean."

She stopped folding.

"The old man.... They were that same crystal-clear blue color."

After flashing a knowing expression, she smiled.

"Good night, Mom."

And with that, he left. Carolyn shook her head at the thought of children and mumbled, "Just when you think you're not getting through to them."

She leaned back in her chair and grabbed one more T-shirt on the top of John's pile. Raising it to her nose, she closed her eyes and inhaled deeply.

So much like Roy. As she continued with the last of the laundry, she realized some time later her smile remained.

***

As John passed his sister's room, an opened door revealed a light that shone near her bed. She appeared asleep. He entered and gently took the

Avengers comic book from her small hands.

Ripping the sheets from her body, she bolted upright. "You told me there were more heroes in the world than villains."

He flinched, surprised she'd awoken. "That's right."

"If there are more heroes than villains, why do so many bad things happen in the world?"

Her question startled him, and he sat on the bedside. "I guess...sometimes...heroes can't do it all by themselves. They need help from others." Grabbing the blanket, he pulled it to Jennifer's chin and gave her head an affectionate pat. "Go to sleep, sis."

She rested her head on the pillow. Leaning toward the light, he clicked it off. As he left the room, he noticed a photograph on her dresser. He placed the comic next to a framed picture of their father. In the prime of his life, Roy struck an imposing military figure.

Jennifer's voice came from beneath the covers. "Good night, John."

His gaze moved from the photograph to his sister. "Good night, Jen." He smiled and closed the door.

Chapter Nine

Mother
August 1, 1945
Somewhere in the Philippine Sea

Twenty-three men held each other in a floating line. The waves softened with the setting sun, and the intense heat that had baked them in daylight gave way to a bone-numbing, nighttime chill. The constancy of waves, moaning, and splashing would carry them through the next nine hours.

Suddenly, a voice separate from the line rose above the darkness and begged for help. "Please...I need a life jacket. I...." The voice, broken and hollow, lingered in the air but continued to rise above the waves. "Please...I'm hurt. I...I'm so tired. I...."

Despite the darkness, the moonlight's

brilliance shone, and the man crying out became visible. He clutched the remains of a deflating raft and floated toward the young sailor as if he were the only one in the ocean. Before he realized it, the injured man swam upon him and grabbed in desperation. His arm was mangled—even in the darkness, anyone could tell. The wounded man struggled for a hold on his neck and looked desperately into his face.

"I don't...have a life jacket. My raft is.... I need...."

He clung with one hand while the other tore a frantic grasp through the water. But the life jacket could not support both men. They went under and swallowed mouthfuls of bloody seawater. Struggling to break free, the healthier sailor pushed him away and fought toward the surface. Again the wounded man grabbed, and again both sank.

"I can't!" he screamed when he surfaced. "My jacket...won't...supp—" Another large gulp of seawater choked him, and he struggled for his life.

"Please! Help me!" the other man cried.

"Get...off!" With one last violent push, the young man freed himself. "You're going...to kill us both!"

Slowly, the other man began to swim away. The remains of the raft were gone, but the haunting voice remained.

"Oh God!...my arm...I'm bleeding...my arm...."

Mercifully, the voice distanced until the man vanished into the darkness from which he'd come. His voice, however faint, remained. "I'm bleeding...so thirsty...I need...I...." And then, it was gone.

The sailor screamed from the line of men. "I couldn't! He would have killed me! He would have killed us both!"

Without warning, a thrashing sounded. No one in the line moved, but all knew the noise of shark intertwined with human. A blood-curdling scream shattered the darkness, and he realized it was meant for his ears alone. The point at which he could endure the cries no more, it ended—nothing, but the serpentine line of men floating in the black water.

Blinking with fear, he clutched the man in front of him with both hands. He thought of his mother and began to sob, quivering in uncontrollable heaves.

Present Day

With a sudden jerk the Old Man woke and sat upright in bed. He glanced at the clock—it had not yet struck 2:00 a.m. Inching to the side of the bed, he rested his bare feet on the cold, familiar ground, stared at the floor, and knew what he must do once again.

Slipping into his robe and feeling every one of his ninety-three years, he moved to the desk.

Heaven above, Earth below. He grabbed a piece of wood and some sandpaper. "And I am somewhere in between," he mumbled.

The wood felt raw and familiar against his wrinkled skin.

Clicking on the desk light, he continued his work. It was his only escape.

Chapter Ten

The Offer

John liked to position himself out of direct view. He strategically sat far enough in the back of the room not to be called upon but close enough to hear what the professor said. And just about every student at Pensacola Community College knew what was being said in that particular classroom. His first lesson in class consisted of the fact that the only sound usually emanating from Philosophy 02006 was the professor's voice.

Megan had told him when he'd first started taking classes how much professors loved to hear *fine discourse.* "And what better discourse is there to hear," she asked with a laugh, "than their own voices?"

On occasion, Dr. Shelly had a knack for

engaging the class with a philosophical seed of debate. She took immense pleasure in watching it grow as she mediated what sometimes became a passionate feud.

John sat, as he always did, between Megan and Steve as Shelly droned on about "the needs of the many outweighing the needs of the few." Mimicking what he heard, he scribbled the same words into his notebook.

"Besides our never-ending quest for truth this semester, I would like to also examine the concept of a hero," Shelly boomed.

Leaving her perch at the podium, she strolled to a desk and leaned against it. "The ancients had their depiction of larger-than-life figures who portrayed great strength and stood as the universal representation for what was admired in their respective cultures. The Greeks? Achilles. The Trojans? Hector. Great heroes, right?"

A young man in the front row responded immediately. "Of course. Achilles was the best of the Greek warriors and responsible for them winning the Trojan War."

"And he was almost responsible for them losing the war." Shelly adjusted her glasses before she continued. "His pride and vanity led him to sulk in his tent while his comrades died in battle. The only reason he fought was born of selfish rationale."

She paused for dramatic effect, a frequent habit. "Can someone else name a hero?"

A girl wearing a *Central Catholic* sweatshirt and sitting directly in front of Steve, spoke. "Hercules?"

"Why Hercules?"

"Because he was unbeatable. He had no weakness."

John sketched a picture of a ship in his notebook.

"Does that make a hero? Having no weaknesses?" Again Shelly paused. "Actually, Hercules did have a weakness, and a rather large one at that. Did you know he suffered from fits of rage that would eventually result in him murdering his own family?"

Several of the students in class snorted with surprise as she made her way to the podium. "Let's move to a more current version of a hero. Anyone?"

A student behind John shouted. "Martin Luther King!"

She pointed to another.

"The firemen who went up the towers to save people on 9/11?"

She nodded and pointed again.

"How about Lebron James?"

Her face melted with disappointment as she motioned to another raised hand.

"What about anyone who fights for a cause or helps people? My uncle works at the food cupboard at the church. Is he a hero?"

"What do you think?"

The student remained in thought as yet another spoke.

"My mom's a hero to me because she raised a family of four on her own and helped to put us all through college."

"So, what's the connection? We have travelled from Achilles to...mom?"

A few students chuckled as a smug smile came to Shelly's face.

"When I was going through graduate work, I was quite poor. I could barely afford tuition, and didn't even have a car. I had to take the bus. It was an hour journey just to get to class. One day, my roommate gives me the keys to her car. She said, 'You need it more than me...here.' For her own reasons, she decided to not only let me borrow, but have her car...free. Was she a hero?"

"No, she was insane!" Steve's words burst the class into laughter.

"Perhaps, but then I must be, too. I am going to make you an offer. I am going to give everyone in here an opportunity to get an A for the semester."

She hooked John's attention. Setting his pen down, he looked up from his drawing.

"All you have to do is perform a heroic act of honor and prove it."

He raised his hand. "What do you mean by a heroic act of honor?"

Shelly continued as if the words were her own. "Auberon Herbert, a nineteenth century philosopher, once said, 'If we cannot by reason, by influence, by example, by strenuous effort, and by personal sacrifice, mend the bad places of civilization, we certainly cannot do it by force.'"

Another pause and she adjusted her glasses once again. "A heroic act of honor is a selfless action that will benefit your fellow man...or woman. Simply put, we need a hero."

The entire class sat, captivated.

"I am going to give you a chance for

fulfillment."

Expressions of incredulity rose from some in the classroom while others rolled their eyes in disbelief.

"If anyone in class donates something of great personal value to charity and obtains the necessary proof, I will give you an A for the semester."

"How about a car? Like your roommate," Steve blurted.

"That's not a bad idea."

"You will give anyone in class an A if they donate their car to charity?" A girl wearing a green sweatshirt tossed her hair in disbelief.

"Yes. Yes, I will."

Megan quickly whispered to Steve and John, "I heard she does this every semester. No one has ever been dumb enough to take her up on it, though."

Noticing the grin on John's face, Steve shot a glance at Megan and back to John. "You're not seriously considering this, are you? John? John...did you hear me?"

Megan picked up the cue. "Are you?" she echoed.

He grinned and began to write in his notebook.

She waited a beat then asked, "What is going

through that thick skull of yours, John Mann?"

Students scrambled for their possessions and began to leave, cutting through her question and signaling the end of class.

He rubbed his chin and stared at the sable words he had just scribbled onto the white page.

USS *Indianapolis.*

***

Waiting in the airport, Sarah sat then stood, checked her phone, and sat again. She swiped lint from her blue dress—one of Jason's favorites. Her hair flowed straight down and there was a single braid on the side, the way he liked, and the way she'd worn it when they'd first met.

Airports had to be one of the most emotionally draining places in the world. People were doing one of two things: reuniting with loved ones or separating from them. Luckily for her, it was the former.

Twisting a strand of her dark hair, a nervous habit she'd started as a girl, she watched those around her. Tears of separation seemed to outnumber tears of reunion on that particular day.

She leaned forward to glance down the terminal...again...and brushed away another piece of lint, when something out of the corner of her eye caught her attention. Her heart jumped. A familiar form emerged at the end of a long corridor. When Jason's face became apparent, she let out a scream and leaped from her seat. He spotted her, dropped his possessions, and ran toward her. After what seemed an eternity of being apart, they melted into each other's arms. The early reunion made them wonder if they were in a dream. Only when their lips met did they know for sure.

They separated, not to catch their breaths, but to look into each other's eyes. And after they kissed again, Jason whispered, "Miss me?"

Sarah answered between sobs of joy, "What do you think?"

"God, you feel good. I think it's been too long."

Both held each other with the tightest of embraces, as if their arms could contain the sea of emotion that overwhelmed them.

Finally, she broke the embrace and tears flowed. "And we don't have to ever worry about being apart like this again. You promise?"

"I promise. Never again."

With a deep breath, she reached up and threw her arms around his muscular shoulders one more time.

"Come on," he said. "Let's get home." They returned to his bags, gathered the belongings and headed down the corridor toward the exit.

"You know you're gonna get sick of me now?" He smirked.

She stuffed tissues into her pocket. "I'll take my chances."

"What about Mom? She doesn't know, does she?"

"She has no idea."

Increasing their pace, they continued to the car, not once taking their eyes off each other. Sarah glimmered with happiness, thankful for tears of reunion.

Chapter Eleven

Red Beans and Rice

Vito's Campus Pizza Shop remained a favorite whenever free time presented itself at Pensacola Community College. John, Megan, and Steve were frequent visitors. An extra-large pepperoni pizza, a pitcher of beer, and a seat at a small table in the corner of the shop became their routine. Ironically, it had been the same table where John first met Megan.

He'd been bar-hopping with some friends getting ready to leave for another tavern and the next adventure. But when he'd seen Megan, he told his friends to go ahead; he was staying.

Something about the way she'd sat with her friends that night, the way she laughed, the way her straight hair fell like a waterfall around her face, had struck him like a kiss from Aphrodite herself. She looked up and caught John staring back. His smile held her gaze, and he knew. A couple of corny jokes later and he lost himself in her hazel eyes. They'd talked the next two hours until he finally worked up the nerve to ask her if she needed someone to walk her home.

Fortuitously, he'd not had a car at that time. That moment convinced him their relationship had to be destined.

"You think they have red beans and rice?" Steve gushed as he picked up a menu.

John's lips pursed as he tried to ignore the question. "Don't start."

Megan searched their expressions, her attention hooked. "What're you guys talking about?"

"You mean your boyfriend has never told you the infamous red beans-and-rice story?"

She smiled at John before drawing out her answer. "Nooo...."

He pleaded with his best friend, "Steve, I'm begging you, don't."

"About a year ago, after an evening of frequenting the local taverns—"

"Thanks, Steve."

"Our dear John has a craving," Steve continued.

"For?" she asked.

He addressed John and waited for a response.

He didn't play along, so his girlfriend repeated the question. "For?"

John inhaled—he knew where the story headed and had no power to stop it. Finally, he mumbled, "Red beans and rice."

"We decide to drive to the only restaurant around."

"The *best* one around," John corrected.

"That serves red beans and rice, Fish Bone Grille."

"But isn't the closest one an hour drive from here?" Megan asked.

"More or less, but it seemed like a good idea at the time. When we finally get there, the place is packed. The restaurant is located at the end of some business cul-de-sac, which made parking a little screwy."

"It made the parking a lot screwy!" John added.

Steve pinched his fingers together and

mouthed the words "a little" behind John's back. "We were trying to figure out where to park because there were no empty spaces. We get to the end of the road it was on and John has no choice but to do a U-turn."

"I didn't see it," John announced.

"Didn't see what?" Megan raised her eyebrow, curious for more of the story.

"The sign."

"There was a sign that clearly said...." Steve waited for John and both exclaimed simultaneously, "No U-turn!"

"And that's when he got us," Steve said.

"Who?" Her eyes widened.

A waiter arrived in a hurry, placed three waters on the table and left. John grabbed a glass and took a sip to wet his lips before he continued. "A copsicle."

"A what?"

"A cop on a bicycle," Steve said. "He pulled us over with some strange little siren and light on the handlebar. I think he was going to just give us a warning, but then again we will never know."

John blushed and lowered his gaze.

"At this point, our dear John made a minor

mistake."

"I was trying to explain to the officer that we were attempting to—"

"What did he do?" Megan interrupted. She tilted her head in worry.

"It's what he shouldn't have done. He got out of the car." Steve waggled his finger at him as if correcting a puppy. "The police officer told him to get back in, and John decides to prove a point. The next thing I know, the officer grabs him, spins him around, throws him against the hood of our car, and pats him down."

"Does your mom know about this?" She cast a worried expression toward John.

"Of course, she does." He took another drink of water.

Steve made eye contact with Megan and mouthed the word "no" behind his best friend's back and continued, "And it was at this point, John decides he has had enough."

"I didn't know what this guy was going to do, so—"

"So, John starts walking toward our car like he wants to get back in, the police officer decides he's resisting arrest and tries to take him to the ground and handcuff him. But first, he needs a weapon!"

Megan stared wide-eyed at John. "A weapon?"

"It's not what you think."

"The officer takes out"—Steve pulled a pen from his pocket and held it high for effect—"This!"

"That?" A giggle escaped her.

"That." John nodded.

"He takes the pen and sticks it into John's ear. I believe he was looking for a pressure point," Steve said.

"And here I thought he wanted my autograph. I don't know what he was looking for, but it hurt like hell."

"So picture this. I'm still sitting in the car and there's no way I'm getting out now, and John, lying on the ground with a cop on top of him and a pen sticking out of his ear, lifts his head to look at me and starts chanting, 'red beans and rice, red beans and rice' over and over again."

"At the time, it seemed like the thing to do."

"And all I can do is laugh in the car and wave."

"I'm glad you found it humorous." John scanned the pizzeria. "Where is our waiter?"

"Before you knew it, they threw him in a paddy wagon and took him downtown...and, John, would you like to continue?"

He took another drink and licked his lips. "I spent the evening in a holding cell with one of the largest men I have ever seen in my life. He had tattoos on places I didn't know it was possible to tattoo. There was only one cot, and he laid on it...passed out."

"And?" Steve begged.

"And...he was dressed *only* in a T-shirt. I had to sleep on the floor, on the opposite side of the room. Needless to say, I really didn't sleep much."

"And the shirt?" Steve prompted.

"He wore a shirt that...." John broke off, unable to continue.

Steve waited for the coup de grace. "Go on."

A wide grin crossed John's face. "The shirt said, 'Have you tried our red beans and rice lately?'"

Steve tugged at John's shirt, urging him to continue. "From?"

"Fish Bone Grille."

Megan reduced into tears of laughter as Steve continued in a serious tone, "It took me a while, but I found where he was being held. I bailed him out with my own money, I might add!" Steve slapped him on the back. "What are friends for? What did they end up charging you with anyway?"

"You spent the night in jail?" Her voice echoed louder than she intended.

"It was a holding cell." John motioned for her to talk softer. "And they dismissed the charges, thank you!"

"Later that morning, we drive to Fish Bone Grill to finally get our red beans and rice," Steve said.

Megan's laugh trailed off. "After all that, I hope it was worth it,"

"They were closed," John said. "They aren't open on Sundays." He grabbed his glass, took a drink, and set it down. "It was a crazy night."

"Not as crazy as, say, giving your car away for nothing." Steve rolled his eyes.

"Are you really considering this?" she asked. "Because if you're just doing this to get an A...."

"Or because no one else has," Steve added.

"Dr. Shelly would say if you're doing it for the wrong reasons, then it's not an act of honor." Megan waited for a response.

"I am considering it because...." John rubbed his chin as if he were Rodin's *Thinker*.

"Go on," Steve urged.

"I am considering it because someone once told me I need to serve others before myself."

Steve searched for the waiter. "Are you talking about the service here? Because if our waiter takes any longer, I'm going to climb over the bar and serve myself."

He stood and walked toward the counter. John grabbed Megan's hand, held it between his, and squeezed, tenderness flowing from his fingers.

He leaned and spoke so only she heard. "I know I've done some stupid things lately."

She gave a knowing smile.

"But I never want to do anything that would hurt what we have. Meg, I need to do this. I don't want to live a life of almost. I am tired of almost. I need to prove to myself there is more to me than people think, more than I have given myself credit for. I want to show others that I'm—"

"You don't have to show others anything. I love who you are, and I know the man you want to be, the man you can be, the man you are going to be, but you have to see it."

A dramatic tone rang in his voice. "Being a man is a hell of a thing."

"Hemingway? Yeah, I was paying attention in

English class, too."

He pulled a strand of hair from her face. "I've gotta get going. I have to get to the retirement home. I'll talk to you later."

"But we haven't had lunch yet!"

"I'll be fine. I'll grab something there." He kissed her on the cheek. "Meet me at the library when you're done with class."

"Of course."

"See you in a little bit. And Megan?"

"Yeah?"

"Whatever you do, don't order the red beans and rice."

Chapter Twelve

1,196

On Tuesdays, certain things could be counted on at Saint Francis. The dining room always served Salisbury steak, sliced carrots, and mashed potatoes. Nurse Nancy would instruct her staff to put a *treat* in every resident's room. Due to recent government regulations, a freshly cut apple provided the snack.

Lately, John collected used lunch trays from residents. A squeaky wheel whined repetitively as he pushed the tray rack through the halls. The sound announced his presence in advance, at least for the residents who could still hear.

Wearing his green Saint Francis shirt and Staff lanyard around his neck, John stopped at the next room on his route and knocked on the door. The room belonged to 89-year-old Louise Johnson. As he entered, a record player crooned Frank Sinatra's "Have Yourself a Merry Little Christmas."

Mrs. Johnson wore thick glasses and sat on her bed, facing the wall next to her. He'd noticed that pastime had become more frequent. Pictures colored in crayon covered the wall. One in particular caught his attention—a Christmas tree decorated with green, red, and white stars with the words *To Gramma* scrawled at the top. The more he scanned the collage, the more he noticed the same salutation.

"Happy Tuesday, Mrs. Johnson!"

She woke from her reverie, spotted a familiar face, and smiled. "Happy Tuesday, dear!"

"A little early for Christmas music, isn't it?"

"It is never too early for Christmas music, or Frank Sinatra for that matter."

"Good point." Taking her tray, he noticed a picture of Santa, complete with an orange beard and sleigh, resting on her lap. It was signed *Love, Alexis.* "That's a pretty picture. Is Alexis your granddaughter?"

Mrs. Johnson delicately held the picture, a distinct sense of pride reverberated in her voice,

"One of five grandchildren, dear."

"Will you be seeing them for Christmas?"

"They live in California. I just don't think it's going to work out this year...again."

Her words froze John, for some day he may be alone, too. The warm, velvet lyrics of Sinatra filled the room with a sad irony. As John's mind echoed the song with thoughts of happy days and faithful friends, the words "gather near to us once more" stung his ears as he absorbed her loneliness. He could only watch as she sat on the edge of the bed, the collage of lovingly drawn images framing her in a myriad of color. *How difficult a life must be without loved ones to complete it.* He'd learned that lesson at an early age but had recently forgotten it.

He smiled. "It's a very pretty picture." As he left the room, he glanced back to see Mrs. Johnson lost in thought, her gaze returned to the wall.

The judge's words in court came ringing back. *You must learn to serve others first.*

"And you never know...." John began. He didn't know if she heard him, so he repeated, "And you never know, Mrs. Johnson...."

She turned back to him. "Never know what, dear?"

"Maybe they will make it when you least expect it." He gave her a warm smile, hoping to brighten what seemed to him an otherwise dreary day. "'Bye, Mrs. Johnson."

Exiting the room, he placed her tray on the rack, wheels squeaking, and continued down the hall.

The sounds of a baseball game emanated from the next room. James Kenney, a bald, eighty-two-year-old black man and dressed only in a robe, sat on his bed. Over the last few weeks he'd worn a black leather cowboy hat, and that day was no exception. The baseball game played on a small black-and-white television perched on a dresser.

"Hello, Mr. Kenney."

"It's about time. You're missing the game!"

"Sorry, I got held up by Mrs. Johnson." John winked. "So, what's the score?"

"Three-one, the Indians of Cleveland." Mr. Kenney took off his hat and wiped his brow, revealing his bald head. "Have I ever told you I used to play in the minors?"

"You told me how you played into your seventies."

"Love the game. Best game ever invented." He

motioned for John to have a seat. "Had to give it up when I started seeing double at the plate. I tried batting with one eye closed, but it just didn't work."

John sat in the corner and listened intently.

"I played senior ball not too far from here. Imagine a bunch of sixty, seventy, and even eighty-year-olds playing baseball. God, it was fun. We had two pitchers die on the mound in '96...same game."

"You're kidding me?"

"No, they really did. The ambulances came, one in the third inning, one in the eighth. We said a prayer each time then finished the game. We won five-two. They would have wanted it that way."

"I imagine they would have." John chuckled as he stood and grabbed the lunch tray. "I'll talk to you later, Mr. Kenney. Got to keep my schedule. Be good!"

"You, too, my boy, and don't forget, keep swinging for the fence...even if it is with only one eye." Mr. Kenney's attention returned to the baseball game.

In the hall, John placed the yellow tray on the rack. Again, the wheel started its song, but he doubted many heard. He had anticipated the next visit on his route throughout the day. The room belonged to the Old Man. Knocking on the open door, he peeked inside. The Old Man sat at his desk and worked on a half-completed birdhouse.

"Mind if I come in?"

The man continued to work. John knocked louder and repeated the question.

A sudden growl emanated from the room, and a distinctive, gravelly voice followed. "Enter."

John worked his way past a row of birdhouses stacked along the wall. This time he actually had a good look at them. They differed, some in a slight manner, others in a more dramatic way, but each unique in its own way. Moving farther into the room, he spotted a lunch tray of half-eaten food.

"So, how's the food around here?"

The Old Man remained focused on the birdhouse and didn't answer.

John asked again, this time a bit louder. "How's the food around here?"

Not sure the Old Man heard him, he was about to repeat his words when the reply came. "The chow is kind of like the nurses."

"Which means?" John chuckled, anticipating his answer.

"Bland and cold."

John reached for his tray, and as he did so, spotted the framed picture of the *Indianapolis* from his first visit. Still half-covered by the newspapers, it sat in the same spot as before.

"So, you served on the *Indianapolis*?"

"Yeah."

"What was your job?"

"I worked in the engine room."

"What was that like?"

"Hot and loud."

"The ship I mean, in general." John's words were earnest yet contained a hint of understanding the Old Man's sarcasm.

He stopped his work and studied John. His piercing blue eyes tore a hole in him as he appeared to search for sincerity. Satisfied it was there, he put down the piece of wood he was shaping and continued. "The *Indianapolis* was a Portland-class cruiser. She was the flagship for the fifth fleet. 610 feet long, she could cut through the Pacific at almost thirty-eight miles per hour, record time back then."

"How long was it before you were engaged in combat?"

"Our first action came in the South Pacific. It

was late in the afternoon of February of '42, when we were attacked by eighteen twin-engine Japanese bombers."

John sat on the corner of his bed, absorbed by the story, when he noticed a tattoo on the Old Man's forearm. The ink pictured an anchor being held by a hawk. "Were you scared?"

"Hell, yeah, I was scared! Working in the engine room is damned loud, but I knew what was going on." The man resumed his work. "I knew what the danger was and when we were in it, but I had a job to do, so I focused on that."

"How did you win the medal?"

He abruptly stopped his work. "Make way, I've gotta get to the head."

He brushed by John and entered the bathroom and urinated.

John rose and examined one of the many wooden lighthouses sitting on top of a dresser.

The Old Man's voice barked from inside the bathroom, "1,196."

"1,196 what?"

"1,196...that's how many men served aboard her. And would you like to guess the average age of the men serving aboard her?"

"Twenty-Eight?"

The Old Man returned to the makeshift workbench. Grabbing a piece of sandpaper, he began to scour a piece of wood. John picked up one of the wooden lighthouse and turned it over in his hands. "Try nineteen."

"Nineteen!" John set the structure down and returned to his seat. "Jesus, that's younger than me!"

"Yeah, and protecting this country you call home. Don't they teach this stuff in history class? Look it up yourself." The Old Man stopped his work. "You do have history in school, don't you?"

"Not this semester."

"Well, for shit's sake," he muttered and rolled his eyes in disbelief. "What do you have?"

"I am currently taking fifteen hours. I have the usual...astronomy, English, math, and a philosophy course. The instructor is offering an A to anyone who donates their car to charity."

"Why the hell would he do that?"

"*She* says it's 'a heroic act of honor' and doing it will prove your worth to humanity, and more importantly, get you an A in class."

The Old Man growled a profanity.

"I'm thinking about doing it."

"Why the hell would you do that? A heroic act of honor? She probably can't spell the word let alone know what one is." Striding over to the window, he peered outside. The sunlight streamed through and exposed the deep wrinkles and age spots on the back of his neck. "Hell, she's probably a 2-10-2!" the man said, a sense of disdain pervaded his voice.

"A what?"

"Never mind." The Old Man went back to his work desk. "Hand me that small paintbrush, would you?"

John searched the desktop strewn with tools, pieces of wood, and various bits of sandpaper.

"The one to your starboard!"

He found it and handed it carefully to the Old Man.

"You love your family?" he asked.

"Of course."

"You love your country?"

"Sure."

"Then show it. That's what is important. That's what is honorable and heroic."

John gave a respectful nod. After a judicious

gaze, the Old Man continued his work.

"Well, I better get going. I have to finish my work here and head to the library for school. I'm supposed to meet my girlfriend."

"I hope she's not a 2-10-2."

John opened his mouth but didn't know what to say.

"Back in the Navy we would describe a woman's looks with numbers. For instance, a 2-10-2...you know what a 10 is right? Well, when we were at sea, a 2 quickly became a 10. And then when we made it back to port, she became a 2 again." The Old Man chuckled. "Get it?"

"Yeah, it's kind of like wearing beer goggles."

The man gave him an inquisitive stare and a slow smile began to form. "Stroh's glows? I guess it is...I guess it is."

He grabbed the tray and made his way to the door. Before exiting, he stopped and spun toward the Old Man.

"You know, you still haven't told me how you won that medal." A low, guttural growl cued John it was time to leave. Slipping out of the room, he began to push the rack.

Suddenly, the Old Man's voice filled the

hallway. "Hey, newb."

He stopped, knowing the next words before they came out of the Old Man's mouth. "Get a haircut!"

John smiled to himself before roaring back. "And for your information, Megan is a 10-10-10!"

In a half-whisper, half-chuckle, the Old Man's reply sounded, "Good answer kid. Good answer."

And the squeaky wheel continued its song.

Chapter Thirteen

Special Delivery

Carolyn's job as a legal secretary filled her day with incoming calls, outgoing letters, upset clientele, and the general chaos an office and bosses can offer. She enjoyed her job, but when the end of the working day came, she gratefully headed home and waited for Jennifer at the bus stop.

The most peaceful time of day for her consisted of the short trip from the bus stop to home. It provided mother and daughter a chance to share the adventures of their day. And Jennifer always had her share of adventures. When they arrived home, Jennifer would sit at the kitchen table and complete her schoolwork while Carolyn chose from a variety of household options.

On this particular day, she started dinner and

assisted with math homework. She had always been the one to help the children with their schoolwork. As she worked behind her daughter, she gazed at her tenderly. The realization that would be the last child she could watch growing and help with homework, struck her. When Jennifer left the house, there would be no more of that, at least not until grandchildren.

A ringing doorbell interrupted the steady hum of quiet afternoon life. Carolyn headed to the front door as Jennifer trailed behind. "Who is it?"

"Special delivery," a deep voice replied on the other side.

Carolyn whispered the words, "Special delivery?" She glanced at Jennifer, who simply shrugged. "Special delivery? I didn't order any—"

"Plumber!" The voice suddenly changed in tone, this time to a higher pitch.

Carolyn's jaw dropped, and her pulse quickened.

"Electrician?"

She didn't recognize that voice either, but did recognize the attempt at humor. She threw the door open, and before her, holding a bouquet of yellow roses, stood Jason. For a moment, she didn't believe her eyes. Almost more than she could bear, she began to tremble at the sight.

"Surprise!" A wide grin beamed on the face of her eldest son. Her mind slipped between what she saw and could not believe.

"Jason! Mom, Jason's home! Jason's home!" Jennifer squealed excitedly. "Jason's home!"

At first, Carolyn froze. An expression of disbelief, excitement, anxiety, and relief rolled into one. It is the face only a loved one of a soldier has upon his sudden return. It struck her like a tidal wave.

Though her stunned head still wasn't sure, she reached for her son, a sudden movement that surprised even him. And when she felt him, she knew. It was real and any gray thought faded.

Standing behind him, Sarah gazed on the scene and watched. Utter joy sprang from her face at the reunion of mother and son. Jennifer squeezed past and threw her arms around her brother's legs.

"Hey, Mom," Jason said. "I'm home."

Bursting into tears, Carolyn clung to him and thanked God for his return.

***

Libraries had always been an enjoyable escape for John. He loved the comfort, quiet and, strangely, the smell of books. He recalled his mother taking him and his brother every Saturday morning. While other children watched cartoons and slept, her children went to the library to pick "at least one good book" and spend the morning reading.

Leaning back in his chair, he grinned at the thought of the very first time he'd entered a library. The enormous building seemed too much for his young eyes. Rows of books followed by rows of books covered nearly five floors and almost 500,000 square feet.

As a child, he'd dreamt of being able to read a book just by touching its cover. He'd wondered how long it would take to run through every aisle, arms extended, "reading" every book in the library. *If only it were that easy.* Jennifer would love to hear about this superpower.

He had work to finish for class, but what the Old Man had said continued to echo in his mind. Reaching for a nearby computer keyboard, he typed USS *Indianapolis*. He clicked on the first link and read the passage.

At fourteen minutes past midnight, on July 30, 1945, midway between Guam and the Leyte Gulf, she was hit by two torpedoes out of six fired by the I-58, a Japanese submarine.

As he read, the passage came alive for him.

The first blew away the bow, the second struck near mid-ship on the starboard side adjacent to a fuel tank and a powder magazine. The resulting explosion split the ship to the keel, knocking out all electric power.

For a moment, he heard the explosions, the screams for help, and general chaos of that fateful night.

Within twelve minutes, she went down rapidly by the bow, rolling to starboard.

John repeated the words as if he did not believe them. "Damn, twelve minutes!"

Of the 1,196 aboard, about 900 made it into the water before she sank. Few life rafts were released. Most survivors wore the standard kapok life jacket. Shark attacks began with sunrise of the first day and continued until the men were physically removed from the water, almost five days later.

John mouthed the words until he found his voice. It cracked with emotion. "Five days? Jesus!" Tears welled, and he slipped his fingers through his hair.

The passage continued, *Five days later, 317 survivors were pulled from the ocean. Many of the crew were lost not to the enemy that sank them, but to the sharks that fed on them.*

Pushing away from the screen, he saw Megan walking toward him. He pivoted from her to put books into his backpack but mostly in an effort to hide his emotion.

"Hey, babe, you ready to go?" He did not respond and she looked at him with concern in her eyes and worry in her voice. "John, you all right? What's wrong?"

He tried to grasp what he'd read. "I thought...I thought I knew what the old man was talking about, what Jason said before he left." He wiped his eyes, and Megan could only listen. "I have been taught these things over and over again. I didn't understand. If I had just known then what I know now.... I'm an idiot." Clearing his throat, he managed half a smile as he gathered himself. "I've got some good news and some bad news. Which would you like first?"

"The good."

"I have a surprise for you."

"For me? What!"

"The bad news.... You have to wait until tomorrow to get it."

"Thanks. Come on, let's get out of here," she said. "Your mom's expecting us."

John grabbed his backpack with one hand and Megan by the other.

As they walked away, he glanced back. An image of the USS *Indianapolis* illuminated the computer screen.

Chapter Fourteen

Thanksgiving Dinner

John and Megan returned to what appeared an empty household. The weight of his pack fell to the floor with a thud as he closed the door.

"Mom, we're home!" he yelled.

Megan noticed first. "What smells so good? Does that smell like turkey to you?" They walked into the dining room. "What do you know, the table is set."

"With our good china...and apparently we're having guests. There are two extra settings. Mom? Jennifer? Where you guys at?" Still no answer came.

"I thought Thanksgiving wasn't for another couple of days." Megan nodded toward the centerpiece. "Beautiful roses! Are those for me? Is that my surprise?"

"Sorry, not this time."

Finally, Carolyn's voice rang out. "John...Megan! I need help in the kitchen!"

Turning to the right, they entered the kitchen. Carolyn worked over the stove as Jennifer stood on a chair by her side.

"What's the special occasion?" John asked.

His mother and sister continued to work. Finally, Jennifer spun to face them. A wide smile engulfed her face.

"What?" he said.

Carolyn peered over her shoulder, her face radiating with an even wider smile.

"What?" he asked again. "What are you two grinning about?"

A voice he had not heard in a very long time sounded from the side of the room, "Well, look what the cat drug in! What's up, little brother?"

John's mouth fell as he wheeled to see his brother with open arms. "Jason! What the hell are you doing here?" He rushed into his tight embrace.

"You know what they say? All good things must come to an end."

"It is *good* to have you home." John pulled

away and examined his face then grabbed a handful of his sandy-blond hair. "For good? Are you home for good?"

"Yeah, little brother, for good."

***

While the rest of the family sat in the dining room, laughing and telling stories, Carolyn stood alone in the kitchen. Closing her eyes, she listened.

Jason's stories, John's laughing, and Jennifer's questions filled her ears. She began to lose herself. *If only Roy was still....* But she knew better than to go there.

A beeping cooking clock snapped her back. She pulled dinner rolls out of the oven and placed them in a basket. Drawing a deep breath, she entered the dining room. "Everybody, it's time to eat. Let's pray."

The family formed a circle and held hands.

"I have waited for this moment too long," she began. "A little early, but a true Thanksgiving feast!"

Faces smiled and heads nodded in agreement.

Carolyn started the prayer. "Bless us, O Lord,

and these thy gifts...."

Her children joined in, "Which we are about to receive from your bounty, through Christ our Lord."

Jennifer continued alone. "May the souls of the faithfully departed...."

And the family finished as one. "Rest in peace. Amen."

Everyone found their seat thanks to the name placards Jennifer had made when she set the table. Plates filled and "Thanksgiving" dinner began.

Jennifer piled mashed potatoes onto her plate. "Jason, I have to know. What's it like to fly like Superman?"

"Well, little sister, I am sure Superman would agree. It's exhilarating." Jason smiled and grabbed a dinner roll to demonstrate. "Taking off like a speeding bullet, I have to get steep and fast. I can rocket up to twenty-thousand feet in just over a minute." He raced the dinner roll past her face.

"Twenty thousand! What can you see up there?" Her voice squealed with excitement.

He pulled the dinner roll back, took a bite, and placed it on his plate.

"Everything. I have seen comets, the Northern

Lights and shooting stars. That's one of the great ironies of flying. You're sitting in such a small cockpit, but the canopy above you opens up to the world. It's almost like a God's-eye view. Heaven above, earth below and I am somewhere between."

"Cool! But don't you feel crammed in there?" she asked.

"There's no sensation of being confined since you can see in every direction."

"What is the most difficult thing about going on your missions?" John said.

Jason tilted his head back and thought for a moment. "We have to constantly be on the lookout for what we call collateral damage...namely for civilian casualties."

"What does that mean?" Jennifer asked.

"It means they try not to shoot the good guys, just the bad." John flew another dinner roll past her face, and she tried to snatch it.

"It takes discipline as we have to use what we call 'courageous restraint,'" Jason added.

"What does that mean?" Jennifer shrugged.

"It means even if someone on the ground is in trouble, I have to make sure I know what my target is. If I see from the air that a school is nearby and dropping a bomb would cause significant damage and possible loss of life, I can't help my friends the way I would like."

***

For a brief moment, time froze at the Mann residence. Carolyn felt numb at the thought of her family made whole again. A sense of satisfaction washed over and filled her with contentment. As she watched her children laughing and sharing their lives, she could never want anything more.

Jennifer began using her dinner roll as a plane like her brothers but dropped it into a pile of mashed potatoes. Gravy splashed and the family burst into laughter. It seemed as if Jason had never left. The conversation continued well beyond the eating.

"All I know is that you are safely home." Rising, Carolyn kissed Jason on the top of his head then grabbed several empty plates and started for the kitchen. "And everyone can help clear this table."

As he rose, he reached over and gave his brother a bear hug. "How about you, John? You staying out of trouble?" He nodded toward Megan and laughed. "You keeping your man in line?"

"It isn't easy." She winked. "But I'm trying. He's getting better."

After John and Jason set their dishes next to the sink, John pulled his brother aside. "I've got someone I'd like you to meet."

"Mom told me a little about him. He's made quite an impression on you?"

"He's reminded me of a lot of things I have forgotten...a lot of things that I think I wanted to forget. Does that make any sense?"

"Yeah, it makes perfect sense."

***

John and Carolyn waved good-bye on the front porch, watching in silence as Jason, Sarah, and Megan drove away. Their taillights disappeared into the darkness.

Carolyn put some remaining plates and pans away in the kitchen as John packed his sister's lunch for school the next day. She watched his actions and realized she hadn't had to ask him to do it.

"John, I want you to know how proud I am of

you. How proud your father would be. I think you are a terrific young man, and I just felt I needed to say it...and you to hear."

He placed Jennifer's lunch inside the refrigerator and went to his mother. "Thanks, Mom. That means more than you know."

He kissed her cheek and began to leave the room, but spun back to her. "For the first time, I think I understand where I'm at in life and, more importantly, where I'm headed."

"The answer has been there the whole time. It's just a matter of finding your true North."

"My true North?"

"Yes. It's something sailors had to do when they were lost at sea."

"Finding your true North always points you in the right direction?"

"Always."

"Good night, Mom."

"Good night, dear."

Leaving the kitchen, John decided to peek into his sister's room. The lights were out, but the glow of a flashlight illuminating Jennifer's silhouette, came from under the sheets. He stepped in, picked up a corner of the bed sheet, climbed under, and lay next to his sister. Superhero comic books surrounded her.

John grabbed one of the comics from the pile while his sister read next to him. The front cover displayed Superman's red cape, tattered, torn, blowing in the wind and hanging raggedly from a wooden pole. He was about to open it when she broke the silence. "Can heroes die?"

"What do you think?"

"I'm not sure. Once, I thought Batman died, but he really didn't. He just fell into a pit. Heroes can't die, can they?"

Pulling the covers back, he began to gather the comics. "Heroes never die."

He placed them on her dresser, very near the framed picture of their father. For a moment, the photograph held John's gaze. He extended his hand and traced the edge of the frame. "They will always live in a very special place."

"Where?" Her tiny voice held the innocence only a child's could.

He pointed to his heart. "Here, Jennifer. They will always live here."

"Just like Daddy?"

From the doorway, he addressed her. "Yeah,

Jen." Glancing at the picture one more time, he finished in a whisper, "Just like Dad. Now go to sleep, sis."

Closing the door behind him, he leaned against it and closed his eyes. John filled his lungs with one deep breath and uttered three words not spoken in a very, very long time.

"Good night, Dad."

Chapter Fifteen

Act of Honor

John's thoughts started to race as his car came to a stop. The judge's words continued to echo in his mind. They had all morning.

You need to serve others before yourself.

John's hair blew in the wind as he stepped out of his 1993 Honda Accord for the last time and stared at the vehicle. Steve emerged from the other side.

He broke the silence. "You really want to do this?"

John did not respond.

"You are sure, aren't you?"

He only smiled, faced the entrance of the donation center, and began to walk. "Yeah, I'm sure."

"You know you're certified if you do this?" His friend chuckled. "Sometimes your ideas are just too big for your body."

The process didn't take long. After being greeted with a smile, John was ushered to a desk. Papers were signed, and he shook the woman's hand. After he handed her the car keys, she gave him an envelope. It contained "the necessary paperwork" Shelly needed.

Exiting the building and into the sunlight, John put on his sunglasses.

"By the way, I need to borrow a buck," Steve said.

John glanced at him as they headed toward the street corner.

"For the bus. I didn't think you'd actually go through with this insanity."

"Get used to it," John fired back. He fished into his pocket and pulled out his wallet. "Here!" He handed him a dollar bill as the bus pulled into the stop.

Before Steve boarded, a huge smirk bloomed on his face. "You think this line will take us to Fish Bone Grille?"

"Don't start." John pushed his best friend

playfully in the back. "Now get on the bus."

***

John sat in class and scribbled in his notebook while Dr. Shelly's voice boomed in the background. His heart began to race. He gathered his thoughts, leaned toward Megan and whispered, "Remember that surprise I talked about? Well, get ready for this."

Her head fell into her hands. "Oh God...."

John drew a deep breath to calm his nerves. The moment had arrived. He raised his hand.

Shelly paused from her monologue. "Mr. Mann, do you have a question?"

As John rose from his desk, Steve pulled out a cell phone.

"As a matter of fact, Dr. Shelly, I do. Remember when you said you would give anyone an A who would donate their car to charity?"

"I do."

"Does that offer still stand?"

"Of course, it does."

"Then I would like to inform you that I have done an act of honor."

The attention of the entire class fell upon him. The instructor straightened her glasses and examined him, a curious expression on her face.

He reached into an envelope on his desk and produced two pieces of paper then held them high for the class to see. "This is a letter from the donation center stating I have willfully and lawfully donated my 1993 Honda Accord. Here is also a receipt that verifies my donation...." He paused like Shelly for effect. "For tax purposes, of course."

The class stared at him. Jaws began to drop. Someone muttered a quiet profanity from the back of the room and a few of the students nearby laughed. Heads swung from the professor to John, as if watching a tennis match. He marched down the aisle and toward Shelly, who froze, dumbfounded. He dropped the envelope on her desk and returned to his seat.

Before sitting, he addressed the room. "And don't worry, Doc, even though I have an A in here, I still plan on coming to class." Winking at the shocked professor, he sat. Whispers and murmurs of excitement filled the classroom.

Steve put his cell phone away and slapped him on the back. "Dude, that was frickin' awesome!"

As Shelly gathered her notes, John noticed a slight tremble in her hands.

"You can go on now, professor," he proclaimed. "We'll wait."

Under the skyline, USS *Indianapolis* (CA-35) with President Franklin D. Roosevelt aboard enters the New York harbor during fleet review, 31 May 1934.

Off the Mare Island Navy Yard, California, 10 July
1945, after her final overhaul and repair of combat
damage. Photograph from the Bureau of Ships
Collection in the US.

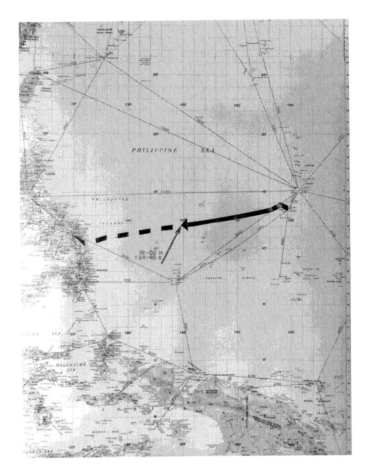

Chart of the western Pacific, showing
Indianapolis's track from Guam to her reported
sinking location, with a dashed extension showing
her intended route to the Philippines. Official US
Navy photograph, now in the collections of the
National Archives.

Indianapolis' survivors en route to a hospital following their rescue, circa early August 1945. Ambulance in the background is marked USN Base Hospital No. 20, which was located on Pelelieu. Photograph was released 14 August 1945. Official US Navy photograph, now in the collections of the National Archives.

An unidentified survivor of the USS Indianapolis
(CA-35) covered in oil and being treated before
immediate transfer to local hospital.
Navy photograph courtesy of YouTube.

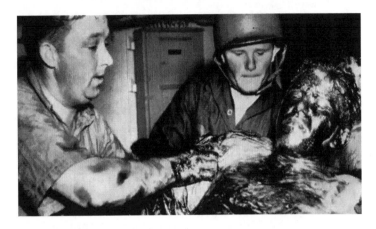

At Sasebo, Japan, 28 January 1946. This submarine
torpedoed and sank USS *Indianapolis* (CA-35) on
30 July 1945. US Marine Corps photograph.

View in the forward torpedo room, showing 21-inch torpedo tubes and three crew members. Taken at Sasebo, Japan, 28 January 1946. This submarine torpedoed and sank USS *Indianapolis* (CA-35) on 30 July 1945. US Marine Corps photograph.

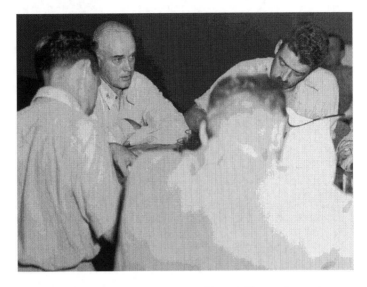

Indianapolis's last Commanding Officer, Captain
Charles B. McVay III, tells war correspondents
about the sinking of his ship. Photographed on
Guam in August 1945, following the rescue of her
survivors. Official US Navy photograph, now in the
collections of the National Archives.

Crewmen holding one of her life rings, circa 1935.
Courtesy of the Naval Historical Foundation,
collection of Vice Admiral Theodore S. Wilkinson,
USN. US Naval History and Heritage Command
Photograph.

Ship's complement and flag contingent posed on the forecastle and forward 8 turrets and superstructure, while anchored at Berth Number One, Long Beach, California, in the last half of 1937. Seated in the front row, center, is Vice Admiral William T. Tarrant, Commander, Scouting Force, US Fleet. To his left, also in front row, is Captain Thomas C. Kinkaid, Commanding Officer of USS *Indianapolis*. Donation of Captain Fred W. Conner, USMC(Retired), 1970. US Naval History and Heritage Command photograph.

Chapter Sixteen

Metamorphosis

John sat in the Old Man's room while he painted an almost-completed birdhouse. His hands worked in a quick and precise manner, a skill developed from years of repetition and practice. He stuck his tongue out the side of his mouth when he concentrated. Neither man spoke. They enjoyed each other's company in a very simple way.

It had been a rewarding eight hours. John had confronted Shelly in front of the entire class, proved to himself beyond a doubt what was heroic, and, as of ten minutes ago, finished his day at St. Francis. He rested his head against the chair and spoke, quite satisfied. "I did an act of honor today."

"Really?" The Old Man started to laugh. "What dumb thing did *you* do?"

"You know that professor I was talking about before and the deal with the car? I did it. In the middle of class, I stood up and told her I'd donated it." He flashed a triumphant smile. "You should have seen the expression on her face! I told her even though I have an A in her class, I'd still attend. And then I gave her permission to continue with class."

His warning tone ominous, the Old Man said, "John, my boy, you'd better be careful."

"Why?"

"There is a difference between knowledge and wisdom. And while your professor may be knowledgeable about the philosophy of her books, the wisdom may be lacking."

John squinted at him.

"In other words, she may not want to practice what she preaches, not to mention I'm sure she didn't like being shown up in class."

"I didn't show her up." John straightened. "She promised anyone an A who donated their car. The whole class witnessed it. And I did it."

"Still, I think it would be wise to be careful with this professor. You know, John, I remember a story about a World War II American destroyer...."

He leaned toward the Old Man and smirked. "And this has something to do with what happened to me?"

"It has everything to do with you if you would try not act like a child and listen."

He sank into his chair. "Sorry."

"The destroyer returned home after a night mission in which they shelled an island occupied by the Japanese. Along the way, they picked up a radar contact that turned out to be a Jap sub cruising on the surface. The sub was unaware of the destroyer's presence because the lookouts were probably fast asleep. The destroyer was going to ram the sub, but at the last minute, the US commander thought it might be a minelayer. And since he didn't want to blow his ship up in the process, they swung the rudder hard to avoid a collision.

"Incredibly, they found themselves sailing side-by-side with the Japanese sub. On the deck of the sub, Japanese sailors were fast asleep. They awoke to the sight of a U.S. destroyer right before them."

John's eyes widened. "Couldn't they shoot at each other?"

"They were so close, the destroyer couldn't lower its weapons and no one on either deck carried a gun. At first, no one knew what to do except stare. The submarine was equipped with a three-inch deck gun, and the sub's captain decided it was finally a good time to use it. As the Japanese crew ran toward the gun, the American sailors turned to some nearby storage bins, picked out the nearest things they could find and threw them at the sailors on the sub."

"What did they throw?"

"They threw potatoes."

"Potatoes?"

"Yeah, potatoes." The Old Man grabbed a nearby piece of wood and lobbed it at John. "I guess it was the spud heard around the world."

He caught the wood, rolled his eyes, and groaned.

"Apparently, the Japanese thought the potatoes were hand grenades because they forgot about the gun and tried to get rid of the 'grenades' by throwing them back at the destroyer. And then, the great potato battle ensued."

"You're kidding me? Didn't the Japanese realize they were throwing potatoes, not grenades?"

"Son, when you are at war and it's dark, and you think the enemy, who is right next to you, is throwing live grenades...you'd be surprised what you don't realize."

"Good point." He set the piece of wood on his desk. "But what may I ask, with all due respect, does this have to do with *my* situation?"

The Old Man leaned back, rubbed his chin and struck a pensive pose. "John, my point is this: sometimes in life, *we* know we're throwing potatoes at people, and it seems harmless. The problem is when we throw them, the people we throw them at may just think they're grenades. Please be careful with this professor. Understood?" He put his paintbrush down and played with his hearing aid.

"Yes, sir."

"Understood?" he repeated again.

"Understood!" John said, a bit louder than before. He watched the Old Man continue to work on the birdhouse. The accuracy of his work amazed him. Despite his age, the man controlled his hands in confident and calculated movements. "Why are you always making birdhouses, anyway?"

"You ready for another story?"

"Does it begin 'once upon a time'?"

"Kind of." After a dramatic pause, he began. "Many years ago...."

John frowned.

The Old Man grinned and delivered a salty sigh. "Very well." He cleared his throat and began again, "Once upon a time...."

John settled into his seat, quite satisfied.

"There was a great battle at sea. After days of brutal fighting, one sailor was all that survived. Adrift in the middle of the ocean, he floated on the remains of his once-proud ship. The man drifted hopelessly, his thirst and hunger tearing at him. Days passed and, despite his hopes and prayers, no rescue came.

"The next afternoon he saw a sunset so beautiful he forgot all his suffering. At that very moment, he made a promise. If the gods would see his safe arrival home, he vowed with every sunset after, he would forever honor them. With death about to claim him, he spotted an object approaching in the sky. At first, he thought his mind played tricks on him but soon realized it was a bird."

The Old Man continued to build, his wrinkled hands working in seamless perfection.

"At the very moment the bird passed overhead, the sailor saw through its eyes—the wreckage below and his own broken body clinging to it. The pain and suffering left him as cool air flowed through his fingers. Suddenly, his fingers became feathers, his arms became wings, and he felt the warm sun directly above." The Old Man paused and reached for a drink of water.

"That's it?" John said.

"No, that's not it! Be quiet!" He set his cup down. "The next afternoon the mother of the missing sailor lay in bed, asleep. She awoke to the most beautiful sound just outside her house—seven familiar notes, repeated over and over. As the woman moved toward the sound, she recognized the melody but still could not place the song.

"When she stepped outside to see where the sound came from, she saw a small bird perched on a birdhouse, bathed in the light of the setting sun. It faced her and continued to sing. Tears came to her eyes as she realized the very birdhouse the little bird perched on was the same one her son had made for her before he'd left for war. And the melody the bird whistled belonged to a favorite song her son used to sing as a boy in church.

"And every evening at sunset, the little bird would sing his song. Word spread throughout the village and people would gather to listen in amazement. Legend has it that every evening as the sun sets, the bird's singing can still be heard at that very spot."

John finally understood. "So, that's why you build—"

"And ever since, families of sailors keep birdhouses in honor of their departed sons and daughters." The Old Man picked up the birdhouse and inspected it. "And if God forbid something were to ever happen, a bird would carry their lost souls safely home."

Placing the birdhouse on the desk, he smiled with a sparkle in his deep-blue eyes. "You want to help?"

In an instant, John saluted. "Yes, sir."

The Old Man inspected him as if it were some kind of naval drill. "You have a steady hand?"

"Yes, sir!"

"Have a seat, sailor."

He jumped to the seat next to the Old Man, who handed him a brush. Both began to paint the birdhouse.

"My dad died when I was thirteen," John began. "My mom works two jobs sometimes just to keep up with the bills. My older brother Jason is a lieutenant in the Navy and my kid sister Jen...she's nine and loves to read comic books."

"Comic books?"

"Yeah, my dad had a huge collection of them when he was a kid."

The Old Man stopped his work and watched him in thought.

John continued to paint then noticed the Old Man staring at him. "What? Did I do something wrong?"

He smiled and patted John on the back, a paternal tenderness flowing from his calloused fingers. "No, son, not at all." They resumed their work, a quiet peacefulness in the air. "Use the white paint on that part."

Chapter Seventeen

Charades

As Christmas rapidly approached, Carolyn couldn't remember the last time she'd anticipated celebrating a holiday quite like this one.

Alone in the kitchen, she leaned against the counter. The aroma of freshly baked chocolate chip cookies hung in the air. John and Jason raced into the room as if they were children again.

"Hey, Mom!" they cried, crashing through the doorway.

She glared, a suspicious eye never leaving them. "Boys...."

John moved to grab a cookie from a tray, and she yanked it away.

"Uh uh." She shook her head. "You know the rule."

John watched helplessly as Jason sneaked on the other side of Carolyn and out of her sight. He grabbed a cookie and stuffed it into his mouth.

"Yeah, yeah. I know," John said, dejection in his voice. "Reject cookies only until Christmas day."

Jason pointed to a small pile of misshapen, burned cookies on a paper towel. "Go to the island if you want a cookie!" Bits of chocolate chip flew from his mouth as he spoke.

"The island?" John repeated.

"The island of misfit cookies!" Jason laughed.

Carolyn gave her boys a smirk, glanced at the tray in her hands, and found one of the cookies missing. Raising her spatula in attack position, she demanded, "Did you?"

John pointed an accusing finger.

"Hey, just realized, gotta go!" Jason ran from the kitchen before Carolyn could utter another word.

John chuckled at his brother's brazenness and rushed into the family room. Checking his computer, he brought up a window showing an auction ending on Ebay and made a bid.

***

Nights like that became common at the Mann household. And Carolyn savored every moment. Dinner with the entire family was as much of a ritual lately, as was the tradition of sharing their day when Roy was alive.

Eating always gave way to story time, and each family member always took his turn. Carolyn smiled with contentment at the scene in front of her. If she hadn't known better, life may have begun to resemble a Norman Rockwell painting.

"And don't forget," John spoke to Jason, "tomorrow we're going to see the Old Man."

"Sounds good." Jason patted his stomach and grinned at Carolyn. "Mom, that was awesome."

"Thanks, Mrs. Mann. You cook so much better than"—Megan showed an empty plate and giggled—"my mom."

"Thank you, dear." Carolyn's smile radiated through the room. "Everyone, the dishes can wait. Let's just relax and enjoy each other's company."

"Mommy, may I have more carrots?" Jennifer asked.

"More carrots?" She raised an eyebrow and stared at her daughter. "Honey, why do you want more carrots? You've already had three helpings."

"Let's just say I heard eating carrots can help you."

John covered his face with a napkin. "Well, of course they're good for you." His face turned red as he tried to contain his laughter. "But how exactly do you think carrots can help you?"

"I heard they can help your...." Exasperated, Jennifer threw her hands into the air. "You know!"

"No, honey, I don't." Out of the corner of her eye, she noticed John hiding his face behind a napkin.

Jennifer leaned toward Carolyn's ear, and, despite attempting a whisper, everyone heard, "X-ray vision."

Everyone burst with laughter.

"So, is it working?" John lowered his napkin to reveal a curious smile. "The carrots?"

"I think so." His sister stuffed the final carrot into her mouth.

"Let's find out!" He grabbed Megan's empty plate to cover his hand and asked, "How many fingers do I have up?"

"Two!"

"You got lucky. How many now?"

"Four!"

"I don't believe it," he said. "You're right." He exclaimed to everyone at the table. "She's right!"

Jennifer smiled, triumph shining from ear to ear. "I told you, Mommy! It works! It works!" She jumped from her seat and ran to the kitchen.

"Where're you going?" Jason yelled.

"To the kitchen to get more carrots!"

Carolyn pointed at John. "You! Be nice to your sister."

Jason glanced at Sarah, who smiled in return. "I have an idea. Let's play a game of charades."

Jennifer ran back into the dining room with a plate full of carrots. "Can we, Mommy? Can we? I want to go first? Can I go first?"

"Yes, honey."

She set her plate on the table and took center stage. Bits of carrots shot from her mouth. "Who am I?" She pantomimed flying through the air, running fast and showing her muscles. "Who am I?"

"Queen Elizabeth!" John said.

"No!"

Carolyn scrutinized her every movement. "A firefighter!"

Jennifer threw her arms into the air. "*No!*" She

pretended to toss an invisible cape over her shoulder and take off as if about to fly.

"Kobe Bryant?" Jason hollered.

Sarah wrinkled her nose. "A lion?"

"A lion? Not even close!"

"Superman!" Megan cheered.

"Daahh! Superman...faster than a speeding bullet, more powerful than a locomotion!"

Jason burst into laughter as Jennifer returned a puzzled expression. "I think that's locomotive, little sister. My turn." He rose and grinned at Sarah. He began to pantomime someone trying to walk.

"Groucho Marx!" Carolyn shouted.

John chuckled. "Who's that?"

"Never mind," she replied. "It's before your time."

Megan jumped into the fray. "Larry the Cable Guy!"

Carolyn raised her hands in defeat. "Who?"

Sarah leaned to Carolyn. "Never mind, it's *after* your time."

"Captain America!" Jennifer squealed.

Jason shook his head, paused and tried a change of tactics. He waddled forward, his hands covering his belly.

"You've eaten too much after Thanksgiving dinner!"

Jason's smile wrinkled.

"Oh, my God!" A sudden spasm of elation shook Carolyn. "You're preg—" She spun toward Sarah. "Are you? Are you preg...?"

Sarah reclined in her chair, placed her hands on her stomach, and tapped lightly.

"Well, that's a pregnant pause if I ever saw one." John chuckled.

"What? She's what?" Jennifer frowned, still unsure of the excitement.

Carolyn rushed out of her seat and yelled, almost knocking the coffee table in her exuberance as she reached for her daughter-in-law.

"I still don't get it!" Jennifer stamped her foot on the ground.

"I'm pregnant!" Sarah reached for her niece.

Screams rang in the room as Megan and Jennifer joined the embrace.

John punched his brother in the arm. "You old dog. You're going to be a daddy." He then addressed his mother. "And that makes you...Grandma?"

***

Jason and Sarah pulled out of the driveway as John and his mother stood on the porch and waved good-bye.

Carolyn put her arm around her son. "Quite a night."

"Yeah, I'd say."

"You're going to be an uncle."

"And you're going to—"

Carolyn shot John a threatening glare before breaking into a smile.

"Have an addition to your family...Grandma."

Mother and son enjoyed the moment before starting into the house. John glanced up at one of the unlit porch lights above the front door. "So, what do you think they'll name him?" He reached for the black light fixture.

"And who says it's going to be a boy?"

Removing the cover, he tapped on the light and waited. He tapped on it again, and it sparked to life. "I just have one of those feelings."

Chapter Eighteen

Little, Little Birdy

With the impending arrival of Christmas, the atmosphere at St. Francis began a slow metamorphosis. Perhaps the emergence of decorations spread throughout the building started it. Maybe the infusion of youth helped, as many children from various schools came to visit. Or perhaps the family members who felt obligated to visit or send cards contributed. Whatever it was, the residents felt it and treasured it nonetheless.

John and Jason walked through the doors, impressed at the sight greeting them. Lights were strewn throughout the main atrium. The plastic plants that had added little color to the room were covered with gold strands of garland and bright-white lights.

Christmas cards hung around doorways, poinsettias littered every corner, and cinnamon-scented potpourri filled the air at the nurses' station. At the very center of the room stood a fifteen-foot Christmas tree decorated with colorful ornaments, silver tinsel, and topped with a shimmering white star.

A children's choir formed an arc in front of the Christmas tree and finished the song "Hark the Herald Angels Sing." To the right, a smiling Mrs. Johnson, who had accompanied on the piano, hit the final chord of the song. The expression on her face was one John hadn't seen in a long time, and as he reflected about it, he didn't know if he'd ever seen her so happy.

The residents filled the room and relaxed in front of the choir. Some clapped, others just smiled, but all seemed in the Christmas spirit. Even Mr. Kenney spread cheer, for on top of his cowboy hat propped a large red bow.

A surprising sight sat before the choir in direct view of the residents. Dressed in a Santa suit, complete with beard, hat, and glasses, perched the Old Man. The suit seemed a little large, but that didn't matter. John did a double take at the unexpected spectacle.

But the chair the Old Man rested on was the biggest surprise. The same one John had seen on his first visit—the big red one that had appeared like it should have belonged in some important library, not quite fitting the surrounding décor. He couldn't have been more wrong.

On the man's knee sat a child no older than eight. Wide-eyed, she took in everything around her.

Mrs. Johnson struck the piano keys, and the choir joined in singing "Auld Lang Syne." Nurse Nancy walked toward John. "Hi, John. Where's your shirt and ID?"

John panicked. "I, ahhh...didn't realize—"

"Relax, John. I'm kidding." Her stern demeanor gave way to a slight smile. "Merry Christmas!"

John exhaled, his voice cracking with relief. "Thanks, Nancy. Now I need a bedpan." He elbowed his brother. "I'd like you to meet my brother Jason."

"Pleasure to meet you," she said.

"You too, ma'am, and Merry Christmas."

John handed her a tray of beautifully decorated

Christmas cookies. "These are for the staff. And please give one of the Christmas tree cookies to Mrs. Johnson. I promised her. My mom gets a little carried away every year. I helped ice them."

Jason glanced at him. He definitely had not helped.

"Thank you, John. That's very sweet of your mom...and of you."

All three watched the Christmas performance. The angelic voices of the children sang in perfect harmony with Mrs. Johnson's piano.

John held a gift-wrapped present and observed every movement of the Old Man. Nancy cast him a knowing glance. He and John had grown very close over the last few weeks. "Not what you expected?"

"Not really. I never quite pictured him as the old jolly one." John smirked.

"Believe it or not, he does this every year, and though he might not admit it, he cherishes it. But the ones who really enjoy it? I think that's obvious."

Jason leaned toward his brother. "You said he was in the Navy?"

"Yeah, he served in World War II aboard the USS *Indianapolis*. You've heard of the *Indianapolis*, right?"

"Of course. It carried key components for the first atomic bomb Little Boy on a secret mission that would eventually be loaded on the *Enola Gay.*"

John added, "Otherwise, there would've had to be an all-out invasion of Japan and it would have cost thousands more American lives."

"Little brother, I'm impressed."

John cracked a smile as the choir finished their song.

"Oh, you haven't seen the best part yet." Nancy pointed to the scene as it unfolded before their eyes.

"What're you talking about?" John shifted the present from one hand to the other.

"Just wait. You'll see."

The little girl on the Old Man's knee whispered into his ear. His weatherworn face could not have been more serious. Motioning *yes,* he replied so all the children could hear, "You want me to call on the birdy?"

An immediate chant filled the room. "Birdy! Birdy! Birdy!"

The stern expression on his face gave way to a hint of a smile. A hushed silence followed, as he played up the moment.

"Very well," he said at last. "Gather around

146

everyone!"

The choir surrounded him while the little girl, enthralled, sat on his left knee. The Old Man placed his right hand on his right knee and extended the index finger, a Band-Aid with a small sticker of a "birdy" wrapped around it.

"Can everyone see the birdy?" When he raised his hand high for them to see, they squealed in excited delight.

He sang, "Little, little birdy, why do you stay? Little, little birdy, why don't you play?" As he sang, he raised and lowered the hand every few syllables. The children studied every movement, amazement in their eyes.

"Little, Little birdy, fly, fly away! Little, little birdy, fly, fly away!" The Old Man threw his hand high over his head and brought it down slowly on his knee just as he hit the last word of the song. His finger rose, and to the surprise of the youngsters, the birdy had vanished. They gasped in amazement.

Catching sight of John across the room, the Old Man gave him a wink. "You see, everyone, the little birdy has flown away."

The girl on his knee seemed concerned. "But where did he go?"

"I guess he's flown home. Do you want to see if we can get him back?"

She gazed into his eyes. "Please make the birdy come back."

The children screamed in unison, "*Yes!* Please! Where did he go? Bring him back!"

He addressed the surrounding choir, "Okay, okay, everybody concentrate. This is going to take a lot of faith! Everyone needs to be very quiet."

They fell into a hush as he repeated the same arm movement and started to sing, "Little, little birdy, where did you fly? Little, little birdy, what do you fear? Little, little birdy, reappear!"

As he finished the last word of the song, his hand fell upon his knee, a single finger exposed. He lifted it and presented it so all could see. The birdy had returned. They stared in astonishment usually reserved for Christmas morning.

"How'd you do that?" one of the kids yelled.

"Do it again! Do it again!" cried several others.

The little girl motioned for the Old Man to listen. He leaned to her, and she exclaimed, "It's a Christmas miracle, isn't it?"

He smiled and placed her on the ground. "Sorry, kids," he began. "Santa has to fly, not to mention it's time to feed Rudolph."

"Stay! Please don't go!" The choir pleaded for more in a cacophony of noise. "You can't leave, Santa! Where did the birdy go? Can you do it again?"

He stood and grabbed his empty red gift bag, as John and Jason approached. "Bye, kids. See you next year. My two elves are going to help me to my sleigh now. Besides, I think they need to clean the mess the reindeer made."

The three men strolled out of the atrium and down the hall toward the residents' rooms as the choir started to sing again. Nurse Nancy smiled at the sight as the Old Man in his Santa suit, sandwiched between the brothers, gift bag slung around his shoulder, disappeared down the hall.

"Elves? And what mess would you be referring to?" John gave him a nudge. "So, Santa, do you have any more Christmas miracles?"

"There's always a surprise in Santa's bag." He chuckled.

"I want to introduce you to my brother, Jason."

The Old Man turned and shook his outstretched hand. "The one in the Navy?"

"It is a pleasure to meet you, sir," he said.

"No, the pleasure is mine."

Jason smiled. "My brother has told me a great deal about you."

The Old Man growled, his deep-blue eyes narrowing on John.

Jason studied the Old Man before saying in a tone reminiscent of speaking to a commanding officer, "I just want to say that I appreciate everything you did for our country."

"I'm glad someone in your family has some good sense." A sly grin crossed the man's face, but his next words removed any question of insincerity. "And I want to thank *you* for everything you have done for our country."

Jason gave him a respectful nod, and they entered the Old Man's room.

"Well, since it's Christmas...." John handed him a wrapped present the size of a shoebox. "I brought you a gift."

He pushed aside some pieces of wood on his work desk, took the present, and set it in the cleared area.

"This should be interesting," Jason said.

"That's what I was thinking." The Old Man removed the wrapping paper, folded it in neat squares, and set it next to the box. Reaching inside, he lifted out a small object.

As the tissue paper fell away, John exclaimed, "It's a sext—"

"I know what it is!" His friend examined the sextant, turning it over and over again in his hands. Placing it back in the box with great care, he stared at the ground, overcome with emotion.

At first, John didn't know if his reaction was one of happiness or sadness.

Finally, John broke the silence as he stammered, "Don't you.... Don't you like it?"

The Old Man drew a deep breath. Tears welled, and he turned away from the boys. "Of course I like it. I love it," he growled.

"I got it on Ebay," John proclaimed.

The man tapped his hearing aid. "You found it in a bay?"

John repeated a little louder, "I said I found it on—"

The Old Man winked at Jason.

"Oh, never mind."

"A gift that points every sailor in the right direction," Jason said.

"I think...." The Old Man wet his lips. His

tongue peeked between them, the same as when he concentrated on building birdhouses. "It's everything I ever wanted. Being pointed in the right direction can't hurt...especially when not much points at my age. Thank you, John."

He beamed. "You're welcome."

"I wish you the best." Jason smiled. "It was nice meeting you...Santa."

The Old Man, his grip firm, shook Jason's hand. "Isn't it time you two finally headed out to clean that reindeer mess?"

The brothers moved to leave the room when Jason bent to examine the myriad of birdhouses stacked against the wall. "I love your birdhouses. You're very skilled."

"I've always been good with woodworking." The Old Man sat at his desk, pointing at his next project. "Just a natural talent, I guess. Maybe one day I'll give you one."

"I'd be honored."

"So, I'll see you soon?" John asked.

"Not unless"—he picked up a piece of wood and ran his finger across the edge to check for rough spots—"I see you first."

Jason broke into laughter, and John rolled his

eyes.

"You take care of yourself, Jason." The Old Man clicked on the light. "And that beautiful family of yours."

Surprised, Jason said, "I will, sir."

"Good night, boys."

As they walked out of the room, the Old Man's voice rang. "Hey, newb!" John stopped and poked his head back into the room. "Nice haircut."

"And here I thought you didn't notice." He jogged down the hall and rejoined his brother.

"You know, he kind of reminds me of...." Jason shrugged.

"Yeah, I know," John agreed. "And his eyes are the same color."

***

Still dressed as Santa, the Old Man took his hat off and set it on his lap. He leaned back in his chair and grabbed the gift box. Reaching in, he set aside the tissue and pulled the sextant out again.

Turning it over and over in his hands, he whispered, "I must go down to the seas again, to the lonely sea and the sky, and all I ask is a tall ship and

Heaven Above, Earth Below

a star to steer her by...."

Chapter Nineteen

Proper Place

To say Roy Mann had possessed a disciplined bearing seemed an understatement. Everything had its place. Jason remembered asking his father one time if he'd seen his lost toy airplane.

"Son," Roy replied, "Don't put something where you can't find it." From then on, every time the Mann family needed to find something, it was most likely found, thanks to Roy's simple advice.

The boys learned their father's example well. With the arrival of Christmas, they were more than prepared. While many families had decorations in a variety of boxes and containers, extension cords tangled and light sets that partially worked, the Mann family operated with precision.

Boxes were numbered and color-coded. Red

boxes held Christmas decorations and each had Roman numerals. Boxes one through twelve correlated to outdoor lights only, all strands wrapped in neat bundles and covered with a plastic sheet before being sealed inside. Replacement bulbs sat in smaller boxes designated with the same number as the larger boxes. Extension cords were given ranks depending upon length and usage.

And to sort it all out, a map, hand drawn by Roy, divided the property into "battle" fronts. The diagram marked the location of every strand of lights, extension cord, ornament, and decoration with complete accuracy.

"John, we need two more extension cords. Give me one lieutenant and one sergeant in Delta section," Jason ordered. "And the sun is setting so we have to hurry."

John made his way around the house toward the garage when he ran into his sister—literally. Wearing a Superman cape, she jumped in front of her brother and blocked his path.

"I want to help."

"Come with me, Supergirl." He entered the garage and picked a box off a shelf that contained various extension cords and plugs and then moved the box to the ground so he could view its contents.

"All right, Supergirl, this is a lieutenant and this is a sergeant. Take these to Delta section, okay?"

"KK." Jennifer took the extension cords and sprinted out of the garage. Five seconds later, she returned. "John, where's Delta section?"

"Just bring these to Jason."

She ran again from the garage, her voice trailing behind. "Faster than a speeding bullet!"

John reached into "XMAS VI" and grabbed the last set of white lights in addition to one sergeant and started for Echo section.

Jason continued his work on the front porch as Jennifer skidded to a halt beside him. "Supergirl, hand me a sergeant."

Giving him the extension cord, she sat and watched her brother. The final moments of the setting sun illuminated him in a golden glow. As he worked, he started whistling, the same happy melody in his mind the day his orders had come to return home.

John arrived from the garage and started to string the last set of lights on a small bush. "Remember how Dad used to decorate the entire yard when we were kids?"

"Yeah, it was usually a one-week process, but we always had the best decorated house in the neighborhood."

"And if there wasn't snow, which there never was, he would make his own with a blender and ice the night before. He would blend ice for an hour just to make enough snowballs."

"And then he would put them in the freezer overnight so they would solidify into deadly weapons."

John finished with his set of lights. "Didn't he put them all in a box and hide them in the yard?"

"Yeah, it had a snowflake emblem on it so he knew which box it was, and then, when we least expected it, he would ambush us." Jason yelled to his sister, "Give me the lieutenant, Jen!"

He plugged the cord in and applied the finishing touches to the display. In the meantime, John disappeared around the side of the house. Hidden under a tree sat a box marked with a snowflake emblem.

"That should just about do it." Jason stood back and admired his work. "How does that seem, Supergirl?"

Without warning, a frozen snowball smacked into his side. Unmoving, he shouted, "You! That's it! Hide, Supergirl. This is no battle for you." Leaping from the porch, he chased his brother.

Jennifer shouted support. "Run, John, run!" A snowball flew past Jason and almost hit her.

Sprinting past her, he stopped and threw another snowball that crashed into the front door. She screamed encouragement, and the commotion brought Carolyn, Sarah, and Megan to the porch.

Jason found his brother's stash, grabbed a few, and took cover behind a bush. Snowballs flew through the air as another stray smacked into the side of the house.

"Please keep projectiles away from our home!" Carolyn said.

Snowballs continued to fly from opposite ends of the yard. Then Jennifer ran between her brothers and extended both arms as if directing traffic.

"Time-out!"

"You can't call time-out!" John slammed his snowball on the ground.

Jennifer straightened her cape. "Why not?"

"There are no time-outs in a snowball fight!" Jason threw one more snowball, just missing John.

"Sure there are!" She put her hands on her hips.

John tilted his head. "Who says?"

"My second grade teacher Mrs. Leaper told us you are always allowed to call time-outs any time you need one."

"Oh, Mrs. Leaper told you that. Well then...it has to be true. Time-out?" Jason pulled a white handkerchief out of his pocket and waved it in the air.

The brothers took two slow steps toward each other with their sister in the middle and simultaneously without warning, started to sprint. Jason picked her up and they dropped to the ground in a heap. John fell into the pile, Gypsy joining from the front porch, which reduced the women to laughter.

Finally, the melee ended and the children unpiled.

"Everyone ready?" Jason reached for Sarah's hand and pulled her into his arms.

John disappeared around the corner to switch on the lights. The entire family gathered and faced the house.

"Now, bro!" Jason yelled.

John flipped the switch, and the house was engulfed in color.

"Wow!" Jennifer clapped her hands. "They're beautiful!"

Carolyn admired the work. "Impressive job, kids!"

"Jason"—Jennifer tilted her head and looked into the sky—"are there that many stars when you fly at night?"

"Maybe there are a few more stars in the heavens above, but *this* is just as beautiful."

Carolyn spoke, her voice heavy with emotion, "Your father would be proud...very proud. We love you all very much."

The family stood in silent wonder until Jennifer grabbed her mother's hand and led her inside. The rest of the family fell in line and followed. Lingering to admire their work, Jason remained fixed, absorbing the scene. His sister's words rang in his mind.

Jennifer is right. They do look like stars.

He stood on the front porch and glanced into the sky. The real starlight broke through.

Heaven above, Earth below....

The words rang in his mind. Out of habit, he

threw his head back, searched the sky, and found the North Star.

Whistling a familiar, happy melody, he entered the house.

Chapter Twenty

Mystery Explained

A chill descended in the morning air as the Mann family entered St. Mary's Catholic Church. The decorated building smelled of incense, red and white poinsettias carpeted the area in front of the altar, and Christmas trees and lights formed a green, pastoral landscape behind. A manger, complete with figurines, sat to the right, each hand-painted by an artist's skilled touch. From the balcony, an organist finished a performance of "O Holy Night" as an adult choir harmonized the final keys in support.

Striding in, parishioners filed into pews well before service began. The Mann family ushered into a remaining empty row. Carolyn loved attending mass this time of year. For her, a divine presence filled her heart with joy. She closed her eyes, listened to the music, and let its peacefulness wash over her. When the next song began, she opened her eyes slowly, as if waking from a dream she did not want to leave.

She lovingly looked at each member of her family. Sarah and Jason held hands and smiled for what appeared no other reason than being together. John and Megan sat next to them, his hand relaxed on her knee, and her head on his shoulder. Jennifer smiled, watching the numerous candles lit around the church, and held her mother's hand. Carolyn had not known contentment in a very long time.

Jason whispered to Sarah, "This song...."

"What about it?"

"I just realized this is the one that's been driving me crazy!"

"What do you mean?"

"I don't know why, but lately this melody has been running through my mind...when I was flying, on board the ship, when I arrived home. And now, I can finally place it."

"How do you know?"

"We had to memorize the words to this song in fourth grade and sing it at mass." Jason tilted his head back, closed his eyes, and began to mouth the words sung by the choir. "When tragedy strikes and hate does abound, miracles will happen and love be found. He determines every need, so open your heart, set yourself free."

"Well, I guess you have a good memory." Sarah smirked.

He gripped his wife's hand. "It is a happy song. Isn't it?"

"As long as I'm with you, it will always be a happy song."

***

As the intentions were read, Megan touched the back of John's arm and breathed into his ear, "You know I'm going to marry you in this church."

He squeezed her hand. "I know."

The lector continued from the pulpit and the last intention rang throughout. "Let us pray for those serving in the military. May they do their duty, and may God protect them and bring them home safely to their families, whole and unharmed."

Chapter Twenty-One

City in the Sky

Though John knew the inside of the building, the grounds of St. Francis were foreign to him. As he exited with the Old Man, they followed a red-brick path that led to some nearby woods. He wondered where the Old Man wanted to take him.

Their strides were deliberate and slow. It gave John a chance to enjoy the fresh air and sunshine.

"There's something I have wanted to show you for quite some time. It's a little farther ahead," the man said.

They meandered through the woods and entered an area connected to the grounds. When the trees cleared enough for John to see, he couldn't believe his eyes. A park filled with thousands of birdhouses sat before him, each structure mounted on a post and each at a different height. The effect created a city in the sky.

At the center of the display, an enormous flagpole towered fifty feet tall. An immense circular flowerbed surrounded all sides. Sixteen benches formed an octagon around a bed of various wildflowers. The benches gave way to a web-work of brick pathways weaving around the posts and birdhouses strewn throughout the park.

The Old Man stopped and drew a deep breath. He raised his head respectfully at the American flag waving quietly in the breeze. "This is it."

"Oh my God! This is unbelievable. You built all of these?"

"Yeah, every one. Let's have a seat, John."

As they made their way to a bench, he gawked in amazement. "I can't get over this. This is breathtaking. It is...beyond belief! How many are there?"

"One thousand, one hundred...." The Old Man moved to sit on the bench.

John finished his sentence in disbelief. "Ninety-six. Of course, one for each sailor on the *Indianapolis*." Sitting beside him, he stared at the celestial city.

The Old Man placed an affectionate hand on his shoulder. "I have been working on these since I left the Navy in '48." He exhaled, sounding depressed. "I hear your hours are almost complete."

"Almost," he said, "but I'll still be around to bug you."

"I just want you to know, John, that I'm proud of you." With heaviness in the movement, the Old Man stood, walked to the nearest birdhouse, and leaned on the post with one hand. "It takes a hell of a man to make a change, to become the man he needs to be, not only for himself, but for the ones around him, and I sense you are doing that."

He reached up and adjusted the birdhouse ever so slightly. "There are going to be times in life when you're going to be scared, and the people around you are scared. Everyone is waiting for someone...someone to step up. It's in that moment you have to make a decision."

"Like you did on the *Indianapolis*? But what you were able to do all those years ago...I don't know if I could. I read what you had to go through. I could have never done something like that."

"And like you, I never thought I could when I was your age." He returned to his seat and gathered his thoughts before speaking. "John, you have to search within yourself. Without fear there can be no courage, without courage there can be no honor, and without honor there can be no heroes."

He stared into the Old Man's blue eyes in silence.

"I was a kid when I went into the Navy. I had no idea what I'd be getting myself into. Sometimes, John, life is going to knock you down. The key is to keep getting up, every time, to keep proving yourself over and over again."

"And you did that. You were a hero. You *are* a hero!"

"The real heroes made the ultimate sacrifice. The real heroes were the ones who never made it home."

"That's not true."

"What's not true?"

"You said the real heroes never made it home. Look around you."

Birds flew everywhere around the Old Man's city in the sky. One landed on the bench next to them. They stared at it as a smile unfurled on his face at the significance of John's words.

"Let's go inside. This old man is getting cold."

Chapter Twenty-Two

Star Bright

The New Year flew by like one of Jason's high-powered jets. And before the family knew it, so did February, March, and April. With coursework at college having come to an end, John found a job stocking shelves at a grocery store. Jason continued his work at the naval base as an instructor, flying training missions and daydreaming of life with his family after the military. The women of the family awaited the arrival of baby Mann with a great deal of eagerness. Everyone kept a vigilant eye on every trip to the store for baby clothes and toys.

Even though John's service hours had come to an end, he still considered himself a regular at St. Francis. He had become, according to Mrs. Johnson, somewhat of a celebrity. He even started a euchre club with the Old Man, Mr. Kenney, and another resident. Mr. Kenney always wore his cowboy hat and talked baseball during every hand.

Residents could always count on seeing John with a smile, brightening their day. The Old Man became so impressed with his improving carpentry skill he let him construct his own birdhouses.

Life was simple and content for the Mann family. They lived well, laughed often, and loved much.

"There are two ways you can look at life," Roy always used to tell his children. "You can act like nothing around you is important, or *everything is*. I choose the latter."

***

The first thing Sarah noticed were the names that came with each can. They sounded more like poetic titles, than paint brands, *Seaside Retreat*, *Star Light*, *Star Bright*, *Enchanted Dreams*, *Sugar and Spice*. Deciding which one for the baby's room posed her biggest problem.

She relied on painting when Jason had first gone overseas, the entire process helping occupy her mind from the separation. She'd once painted the living room five times before moving on to the bathroom. And that took *only* four coats. The problem that presented itself with Jason's return was which color to choose, but, with his help, she settled on *Star Bright*.

Wearing a paint-splattered *Fish Bone Grille* T-shirt, Sarah grabbed a brush. Her belly protruded quite dramatically as she was well into her second trimester of pregnancy.

Jason worked from a ladder, ready to finish the trim above the window. When the phone rang, Sarah answered in her usual happy fashion.

"Mann residence!"

"How'd it go honey?" Carolyn asked.

"Well, we just got back."

"And...."

"The ultrasound went fine. The baby is completely healthy."

"Oh, thank God!" Carolyn said. "And...."

"And the doctor knows, but we don't want to."

Jason arrived at her side, paintbrush in hand, and leaned toward the phone. "We want it to be a surprise." Gypsy barked happily in the background.

"That's the way it's supposed to be. All right,

honey. You take it easy. Don't overdo it."

Jason yelled, "'Bye, Mom. Time to get to work! Love you!"

Sarah echoed his message. "Love you. Talk to you later. 'Bye now."

***

Carolyn glanced up just in time to see John enter the kitchen with his backpack. He set it on the table, gave his mother a quick kiss on the cheek, and opened the refrigerator to search for a snack. Not seeing anything to his satisfaction, he closed the door, and spotted the mail lying next to his pack. He leafed through the various letters until one caught his eye—a letter from Pensacola Community College.

"Supergirl! Come into the kitchen. I've got a surprise."

"What is it, honey?" his mother asked.

He smiled. "I just thought it would be nice to share this moment."

Jennifer ran through the doorway with her cape on as he produced a letter for all to see. "What is it? Is it a letter from Iron Man?"

173

"No."

"Is it a letter from Wonder Woman?"

"No, it's better than that...well, maybe."

He opened the envelope. "I have worked very hard for this report card." In haste, he pulled out the contents and read them. Dropping the letter to the floor, he fell into a chair. "I don't understand," he said, his voice defeated, almost broken.

Carolyn picked the letter off the floor. "What is it John, what's wrong?" She read the paper. "This is an excellent report card. You have all A's and B's except...."

His voice rose. "Except for the D- in philosophy!" He headed for the door.

"John, you should be very proud of this." She tried to console him. "You have done—"

"I have done nothing wrong! This woman is the very one that preaches truth and honor and then does this!" Distraught, he continued, "Mom, I'm telling you, I had a grade no lower than.... She told the entire class she would give me an A. She did this"—he stormed out of the room, his voice trailing—"to prove a point."

Heartbroken for him, Carolyn called, "John, come back. John!"

174

Chapter Twenty-Three

Sixty-Year Silence

After an evening of painting the baby's room with a second coat of *Star Bright*, Sarah went to bed and, with Gypsy on the floor next to her, fell asleep while Jason cleaned the paintbrushes.

He climbed into bed after midnight, put his arm around her, and felt her pregnant belly underneath his fingers.

"Good night, Sarah." Leaning over her belly, he sighed as a perfect contentment overcame him. "Good night, baby Mann."

***

He slept until early the next morning. Realizing what time it was, he jumped from bed and silenced the alarm before it rang and woke Sarah. A quick peek out the window revealed nothing but darkness. Soon, he would receive the entire weather forecast at the base for the day's training mission.

He glanced at her, smiled, and returned to bed. *Just five more minutes.*

He enjoyed the warmth of her body and smell of lavender in her hair. Inhaling deeply, he whispered, so as not to wake her, "I had a dream last night. The entire family was in it. You...Mom...John...Jennifer...even Dad was there...and everything was golden...light was everywhere...it was all golden and we were celebrating. I remember now...it was a party...for our son."

He bit his lip, rolled onto his back, and spread his arms wide, one draped over his wife, who continued to sleep. "I was there, but it was like...I was watching...from the outside, and there was the most beautiful music. It was quiet, but it was always there, like a song you can't get out of your head. The sun was setting behind me; I could feel its warmth...and everything was lit in golden light. The kind of light that makes you feel everything is right with the world."

Rolling toward his wife, he ran gentle fingers through her hair. "And as I watched everyone, I kept hearing music, a melody...over and over. And even though I was outside looking in...we were together...our family was...together."

I sound crazy. Let her sleep.

Rising, he went to the closet to dress. When he finished, he returned to Sarah and sat on the edge of the bed. Taking a breath, he watched her. With the most delicate touch, he pulled a piece of hair from her sleeping face.

More beautiful than ever.

He leaned forward and kissed her on the cheek. As he stood, he pulled the bed quilt over her bare shoulders, and went into the kitchen to prepare a cup of coffee. Gypsy followed, wagging her tail, anticipating a treat.

As he waited for the coffee to brew, he began to whistle, and, grabbing a pen and some sticky notes, he began scribbling on each one.

Twenty minutes later, he arrived at the base.

***

John woke and could not go back to sleep. Too

many thoughts ran through his mind, and he decided to pay the Old Man an early-morning visit.

As he moved through the halls of St. Francis, he headed first toward Mrs. Johnson's room. Nurse Nancy had told him she celebrated her ninetieth birthday, and he wanted to wish her well. Approaching her room, he paused.

Strangely, there were no sounds of Sinatra or Crosby coming from within. Only laughter and voices emanated.

He peeked inside to see her surrounded by five small children. She glanced up and waved, her hand conveying a youthful enthusiasm. "These are my grandchildren, John."

"They're beautiful. Happy Birthday, Mrs. Johnson!" He smiled and continued to the Old Man's room.

He found him reading an article from a yellowed newspaper. "Not making birdhouses today?"

"No, son, not today."

"What are you reading?"

He handed John the aged newspaper.

"This is from 1945! This is—"

"The day our story was first reported."

John read the story then set it down. "By the way, you were right."

A distinctive growl followed. "About?"

"You told me to be careful. I should have listened."

Grabbing the newspaper, the Old Man tossed it on his desk next to a few pieces of wood nailed together, the apparent beginning of a new birdhouse.

"I got my report card. All A's and B's except for one class. Would you like to guess which one?"

The Old Man grumbled his response. "Philosophy?"

"Philosophy."

"John, sometimes there is no lesson to be learned. Sometimes things just happen and they're wrong, and that's just the way it is."

"You were right. You warned me. I got her, and she got me. I just never guessed.... Anyway." He took a piece of paper out of his pocket and handed it to the Old Man. "I was surfing the Web last night and I came across this. I printed it out for you."

The Old Man tapped his hearing aid in an obvious attempt to lighten John's leaden mood. "Isn't it a little cold to be surfing?"

He managed a feeble smile. "Anyway, I found this and I thought you might be interested. There's going to be a reunion for survivors of the USS *Indianapolis* at the site of the memorial. According to this article, it's going to be a pretty big deal. It's coming up pretty soon, though. I just thought you'd be interested."

The Old Man scanned the paper and went to the window. Leaning his forehead against the glass pane, he stared outside without a word. Finally, he turned to John. "I know you've asked about it. More importantly, I'm ready to tell you about it." He peered across the room then into John's eyes. "You want to know what that medal is for? You want to know what really happened when our ship went down?"

John nodded.

"What I am about to tell you...I have never told anyone in sixty years."

***

Sarah, belly protruding below the hem of her T-shirt, slipped out of bed to answer a ringing phone. "Hello?"

"Hey, honey. Did you sleep well?"

"Jason, why didn't you wake me before you left?"

She moved into the kitchen. As she continued her conversation, she walked to the refrigerator. A sticky note declared *Love you!* She glanced toward the coffee pot, and then to a kitchen cabinet. With every new note a new message spoke to her. *Miss You! See You Soon! Hug The Baby For Me! Kiss Gypsy For Me!*

"You seemed so peaceful, and let's face it, you and the baby need as much rest as you can get."

Wrapping an arm around her swollen middle, she grabbed another note and read it. "I got your note."

"Don't you mean notes?"

"You know what I mean. Thank you. I love them, all of them." She grinned. "So, everything's going well this morning?"

"Real well. I've got a low-level training flight with a newbie. We're bound for Chattanooga. Should be pretty routine."

"Please be careful, as usual. And tell that newbie he's hauling precious cargo!"

"Of course. I just wanted to call and tell you I

love you, miss you...as usual."

"I love you, too."

"I'll give you a call when we land. Talk to you soon."

"Be safe." She set the phone on the counter and grabbed a coffee cup. On the backside of the cup, another sticky note appeared. She peeled it off and stared at it, smiling.

Giving the note a soft kiss, she pressed it onto the refrigerator next to the ultrasound picture of baby Mann.

The words *Kiss Me!* stared back.

***

Even though the curtains were open and the morning sunlight should have been streaming, a disconcerting darkness descended outside. The wind began to howl. The Old Man clicked the light on at his work desk and it succeeded in casting an eerie shadow covering half his face.

Drawing a deep breath, he began, "When the first torpedo struck, I was sleeping topside. A crashing boom unlike anything I've heard before bounced me up and down. It felt like my ears exploded and my eyes were ready to pop out. I knew. It had to be a torpedo. A few seconds later, there's another."

He reached for a cup of water on the desk, took a long drink, and clung to the cup with both hands. "I put my life jacket on. By that time, the ship had flipped on its side. I made my way to the deck, where men were scattered everywhere in confusion. Everything was on fire. The smell of burnt flesh and hair hung in the air like death. We didn't need a doctor; we needed a coroner. Before I jumped into the water, I had to push two buddies in who were afraid to jump. They were just standing there screaming that they were going to die."

A sudden clap of thunder startled John, and he glanced at the window. The Old Man coughed slightly, took a sip of water, and continued, "When I hit the water, vomit, burning oil, and sailors littered the sea."

"Vomit?"

"As men were jumping in, many swallowed a lot of sea water and the fuel that covered it, which caused them to vomit. One of my friends got tangled in the lifeline as the ship began to sink. He lost his pants, but somehow made it back to the surface. Some men never made it to the surface. They were caught in the suction of the sinking ship and the ocean became their coffin."

John sat unmoving, spellbound by the mariner's tale.

"The men who had it the worst were those who never made it out of the ship because we had to dog the hatches."

"Dog the hatches?"

"Dogging the hatches means the compartments were closed and secured with a metal pin from topside." The Old Man set the cup of water down, some of its contents splashing onto the desk. His hands were trembling, something they never did. "They're sealed and can't be opened in an effort to try and slow the sinking of the ship. There were men still down there in the compartments...and we knew that was the place they were going to die. And they knew...they knew the only way to save the others had to be...to give them more time. For a few precious seconds, they paid with their lives."

Grabbing a piece of wood, he rubbed it over and over against his wrinkled hands as if he could sand it with his flesh. Outside, the storm raged and thunder shook the building.

"The needs of the many," John muttered.

"We tried to float in groups, but.... And we tried to stay together, but soon became separated." A lightning flash illuminated his entire face. Leaning his head against the back of his chair, he closed his eyes and clutched the wood against his chest.

"Their screams still echo through me today." His eyes blinked open, full of fear. "Grown men crying for their mothers, girlfriends and wives.... It was so dark, no one to hear us, but...." For a moment, John thought the Old Man might not continue, but then he muttered, "Just tears in the rain." Gathering himself, he resumed. "After a few hours, the shark attacks began."

"Did you think the Navy was on the way to save you?"

"We were optimistic, but no one showed up." The Old Man set the piece of wood on the desk and wiped his eyes. "In a sad twist of fate, our *secret* mission made sure no one knew about us." He stared through John and out the window as if focused on a passing apparition. "A few of the men were on rafts, some were on floater nets. I'd count myself as one of the lucky ones just to have a lifejacket. There were some who didn't even have those. The best way to keep the sharks away was to stay in groups. I also tried to stay away from the burning and bleeding."

"Were there a lot of sharks?"

The Old Man gave him an awkward smile. "Well, we were in the water, and there was a lot of blood."

"Yeah...bad question."

"The nights were cold, and the days scorched us. We used the oil on the water from the sinking ship to cover ourselves for protection from the sun. All it did made us look like the shadows that stalked us from below. We floated five days before we were rescued. There were 137 in my group when we went into the water...128 died. The Navy court-martialed our captain, Captain McVay, because it deemed his actions negligent."

"But didn't they dismiss the charges?"

"They did, but it was too late. The damage, as they say, had already been done." The Old Man grabbed another newspaper from the pile and tossed it toward John. "He took his own life in '68."

He examined the newspaper and recognized a picture of McVay. "All that time in the water and you were never bitten by a shark?"

"I never got bit." The Old Man paused. "But fear consumed me. It was the only thing that kept me alive. Fear allowed me to...." His voice broke and he began to sob. "Win the medal. You want to know what I did that's so heroic? I survived. That's all."

John spoke, disbelief in his voice, "No."

"The truth is, John, the real heroes never made it home. I should have been in the engine room. I-I was too afraid to give another sailor my life jacket."

"What're you talking about?"

The Old Man's voice heightened, as if the terror from sixty years ago tore at him again. "He pleaded with me, and it was obvious he was badly hurt. He didn't last five minutes without my help. I should have—"

"No. That's not true. No. You did the best you could."

Tears rolled down his pale checks, and his arms moved in wild gesticulations. "We were on the edge. And now, sixty years later, I am still tortured. The men still out there, they're the heroes."

"But you *are* a hero! Don't you remember what you told me? Without fear there can't be courage. Without courage there can't be honor, and without honor there can be no heroes."

In desperation, the Old Man wailed, "Please, John, just leave. I don't want to think about it anymore. I'm tired and—"

"It's okay that you were afraid. We are all afraid at times. I can't imagine—"

"Please, John. Enough! Just go...go!"

"And drawing on your fear gave you courage. It allowed you to do what was honorable. It allowed you to.... You can't be brave without fear!"

The Old Man rose and glared as if his soul hung in the balance. Finally, he cried with all his being. "All I did was survive!" He threw his arms into the air, where they hung, outstretched and suspended. "That's it! I should have given him my.... Get out of here!" John recoiled as the man screamed into his face, "I said get out! *Now!*"

"But...you—"

"Enough! Just go. *Go!*"

The Old Man fell into his chair, desolation in every tear. His hands began an uncontrollable shaking that coursed through his entire body, and John fled the room.

Chapter Twenty-Four

Half Way Home

As the T-39 perched on the Chattanooga runway, Jason could not help but think of Sarah. He kept a picture of her, always in the left side of his flying jacket. Appropriately enough, the picture rested just above the very place she had stolen many years ago. He patted his jacket to reassure himself it was there. No matter the mission, having it always helped.

Soon, the two Pratt & Whitney engines would fire, and he and his crew would be cruising at a speed of five hundred miles per hour. He wished the plane could go five times faster on his return, but this would have to do. As the plane sat refueling, he pulled out his phone and called Sarah. He always did before a flight home, and she would have it no other way.

"Hey, honey, it's me again." Rain began to fall on the runway.

"Are you getting ready to head home?"

"Yeah, we're at the half point. Right now, we're in Tennessee."

"How's the weather?"

"Fine, shouldn't be a problem. Please tell me you're taking it easy this morning."

"Kind of. I decided to paint the baby's room one more time."

"It needed another coat?"

"You know me. I just felt restless."

"Yeah, I know you. You're something else, Sarah Mann!"

"I'll take that as a compliment. Thank you."

"We're going to be taking off shortly. I'm going to demo something for our ensign on the way home, so at least I get to sit up front."

"The next time we talk, I want to hear two words."

"Love you?"

"No, safely landed."

"Of course."

"Thanks for calling. Be safe...as usual."

"And, Sarah, one more thing...."

"Yeah?"

"Give the baby my love."

"I already have."

***

The sudden pounding on her door startled Megan. She stumbled over a stack of textbooks as she made her way through the apartment.

"Meg...it's me...lemme in!"

"All right, all right, hold on."

At the urgency in his voice, she threw open the door. He entered, soaked from the pouring rain. "John, what is it? What's wrong?"

"I was at the nursing home. He told me to leave, Meg. I didn't know what to do."

"Why would he tell you to leave? He loves you."

"He told me the story...about the medal...and everything that happened to him after the ship went down." Distraught, John spun away. "I thought I understood, Meg, but I had no idea what he went through, what any of them went through, what it was really like."

She grabbed his hand and pulled him into her

arms.

"He was so upset. He told me to leave, to get out!"

She held him and tried to calm him. "Give him some time. He just needs some time to himself."

"I thought I understood. I just thought...." He sucked in a quick gulp of air and tried to gather himself. "I don't know...maybe you're right."

She cupped his head and reassured him, "Of course, I'm right."

He inhaled deeply and caught the scent of perfume on her wrists. His breathing began to slow.

"You'll be fine. He'll be fine. Perhaps you could spend a little time with me?"

She embraced him again and whispered, "I think I know how to make you feel better." With the softest touch, her lips kissed his neck and her hands could feel the muscles in his back relax.

"That's a little better."

He pointed to the other side of his neck. She kissed it.

"Okay, that's better, too."

Megan waited as he pointed to his forehead. "Here?" She kissed it and John broke into a smile.

Pointing to his chin, he said, "Yeah, that's

pretty good, too."

Caressing her cheek, he lowered his lips for hers and lost himself in her hazel eyes.

***

After the baby's room had received its third and final coat of paint, Sarah set the roller down. Bits of paint splattered onto the tarp. She moved to the ladder and sat on one of the steps. Gypsy got up from her carpet, lumbered across the room, and licked her paint-covered fingers, her tail wagging as usual.

Rubbing the dog's furry head, she gazed into her eyes. "I know," she said.

Gypsy licked her face as if to say she knew, too.

Sarah peered across the room at her cell phone. It sat silently on top of a tarp covering the crib. Finally, she tired of waiting for it.

As she moved out of the room, the dog followed. "C'mon girl, I'm sick of painting, too!"

Chapter Twenty-Five

I'm Sorry

Though the T-39 Sabreliner could hold nine people, crewmembers always seemed cramped in the tight-fitting plane. Jason sat snugly in the cockpit, next to the senior pilot. Directly behind, the instructor navigator sat beside a student navigator, an ensign about to complete his first training mission.

The engines hummed with perfection as the plane cruised above cloud level, making its way home. The crew had a few minutes to relax before their low-level training would continue and Jason could demonstrate for the ensign the intricacies of turn points.

"I don't know about you guys, but when my duty is done, I'm moving to Hawaii," the navigator said.

"Hawaii?" asked the ensign.

"Yeah, he wants to be a professional surfer." The senior pilot chuckled.

"Get the hell out of here!"

"No, he really does." The senior pilot adjusted the throttle. "I thought you didn't even like water."

The navigator stared, wide-eyed. "For Christ's sake, I'm in the Navy! I practically grew up in the water. C'mon, dude."

"Well, when this dude is old enough to retire, I'm moving to Denver," the ensign announced proudly. "Clean air, good people, and lots of skiing."

"It seems to me you've got a little ways to go before you think about retirement." The senior pilot glanced at Jason. "But you guys haven't heard the best one yet. Tell 'em what you want to do, lieutenant."

"What?" The navigator leaned between them. "What do you want to do when you retire, lieutenant?"

"He wants to be Herbie," the senior pilot said.

The ensign gaped. "He wants to be Herpe?"

"*Herbie.* You remember the Christmas special?" The senior pilot glanced at Jason. "He wants to spend his time in people's mouths."

"Yeah, well, that's one way of putting it, I guess." Jason laughed.

"A dentist?" The ensign rubbed his chin and grimaced as if he were about to have a tooth extracted. "The sound of that drill alone creeps me out."

"Did you know dentistry has been around since about 7000 B.C.?" Jason turned to the ensign. "And for the record, his name is *Hermey*! Not Herbie...and definitely not Herpe!"

"Now *that* is something I have always wanted to know." The navigator double-checked the onboard systems. "Maybe if I had a date with Alex Trebek."

"All right, boys"—the senior pilot gripped the control wheel with both hands—"let's get started."

The crew snapped to a military efficiency. They ran through their low-level checklist as the ensign tried to absorb the protocol.

"Let's go ahead and start our decent to two-thousand feet." The plane responded in an instant to the senior pilot's touch.

"I'm going to be demonstrating a tactical air navigation system, a TACAN point-to-point," Jason began. "Always remember to lead all turns on airways and direct routes, including point to points."

"Yes, sir." His face willed with intent concentration, the ensign noted Jason's every word and movement.

Without warning, a terrible shudder coursed its way through the plane.

The master caution-warning panel began to sound, and a yellow caution light illuminated an ominous indication—low fuel pressure.

Jason silenced the alarm as the senior pilot pulled on the control wheel to steady the plane. "You see something with one?"

"There's a problem with the turbine inlet temp."

Jason manipulated a couple of controls. "It's off autopilot.... What's going on here? Number one is—"

The senior pilot spoke, unexpected urgency cutting the air, "Number one is going to shit. Fuel flow just went to shit."

"Now indicating low oil pressure." The navigator scanned the instruments.

"That shows," Jason confirmed. "Both of

these!"

"They're both going to shit!" the other pilot repeated.

Jason glanced at him. "I don't understand. Air speed should be up, RPMs should be up."

A strong vibration reverberated again as the navigator moved to the middle of the plane and looked out the window to try and get a visual. "Yeah, I'm feeling it, but I can't see anything."

"That's not good." Jason shook his head in frustration.

"You're losing RPM," the ensign said. "You're losing RPM on number one!"

The crew's attention moved to the overhead panel and the master warning light's new threat, a red glare.

"Now what?" Palpable stress shot through the ensign's voice.

The senior pilot pointed at a gauge. "I am now indicating a fire in number one."

"Confirm fire in number one. Let's initiate emergency checklist and start heading back." Jason grabbed the manual and ran through the list.

The pilot nodded and silenced the alarms. "Now moving throttle to idle. Pulling number one back."

"Atlanta NAS, Crusader thirty...." Jason waited for the control tower's response.

"Fire handle pulled," the senior pilot added.

A voice broke through from the control tower. "Crusader thirty...go ahead."

"Crusader thirty would like to declare an emergency at this time. We've shut down number one engine."

"Number two's going." The senior pilot shook his head.

"This isn't right."

"We've lost fuel flow on, ahhh...number two. It's still going through, isn't it?" the navigator asked.

"Atlanta NAS, looks like we're losing number two."

"Four souls on board," the senior pilot said, a grim tone ringing in his words.

"Crusader thirty...ahh...where do you want to go?" the control tower asked.

Jason responded without indecision. "Nearest base."

"Anywhere," the senior pilot snapped.

"Isn't 1B: Robins probably the nearest?"

"Yeah."

The navigator confirmed, "Robins, yes, Robins."

"Crusader thirty cleared to 1B: Robins field via direct. Roger."

Jason strained to remain calm. "Okay. I think we have an electrical problem now, guys."

"Right, we're losing...losing power on...ahh...number two," the senior pilot said.

Jason flicked another switch in frustration. "No, we have to lower the nose. We have to lower—"

The plane lurched again as if a giant hand swatted at an unsuspecting fly. The warning lights and alarms echoed throughout, casting everyone's face in red and yellow hues.

"Goin' down!" Jason said. "We've to put her...there. No civilian population."

"Oh my God."

The crewmembers braced for impact.

"Oh shit!"

The senior pilot tightened his grip on the yoke and shouted to Jason, "Okay, give it all you got! Give it all you got!"

"Crash landing! We're going down. Prepare for impact!"

The plane lurched as if gasping for a final breath.

Jason put his hand over his heart one last time, feeling the picture under his jacket. The thought of never seeing his unborn child rushed through his mind.

"I'm sorry, Sarah. I'm sor—"

Chapter Twenty-Six

In Hiding

The streets were empty as the car made its way across town. It was late, but John didn't bother to know how late. The radio played Pearl Jam's "In Hiding" in the background. Watching Megan drive with one hand, he held the other and wondered why songs from that band always made him feel better.

As they drove through the night, he couldn't stop thinking of the Old Man and his story of the *Indianapolis*.

Megan has to be right. He just needed time to sort his emotions and pain.

She stopped the car on the street in front of his house.

"Thanks for doing what you always do," he said.

"What's that?"

"Making me feel better...and for the ride."

"No problem. See you tomorrow?"

"Yeah, see you tomorrow. Drive safely." He leaned over, grabbed her chin with his thumb and forefinger, and kissed her on the lips. "You're the best."

She smiled. "I know." It lifted his spirit even more.

He stepped out of the car, closed the door, and looked at her through the window. For a moment, John held her gaze. Strangely, the memory of the first time they'd met at Vito's crossed his mind. She shifted the car into drive and disappeared down the street.

He headed toward the house and into the yard. Two men in military uniform were getting into a vehicle that sat parked in the driveway, but he didn't think much of it as they backed out and drove away.

Must be friends of Jason.

He opened the front door and, despite the late hour, most of the lights were still on in the house. He assumed his mother had a late-night cleaning session and wanted to say good night.

"Hey, Mom, I'm home! Sorry I'm late. I just lost track of.... Mom? You in the kitchen?"

He found her sitting at the kitchen table, her back to him when he entered. He went to the refrigerator to search for anything appetizing. "Mom, did ya hear me?"

Without answering, she rose, almost trance-like, opened a cabinet, and pulled out a glass.

"Mom, what's up? What're you doing?"

She reached for another cabinet and pulled a bottle of Tito's from a shelf.

"What the hell? Mom, what's going on?" Heart pounding, he closed the refrigerator door. "Who were those two men that just left?"

"Those two men...." Her voice broke. She simply stood and shook her head. Finally, words burst from her throat. "Those two men were here to...." But again her words broke off and she stared into nothingness; a complete hollowness consumed her gaze. Pouring the glass half full of vodka, she took a deep drink and focused on the glass in her hands. "A training mission.... First Roy, and now...."

"Mom, what're you doing? You haven't had a drink since Dad.... Mom, what are you talking about?" He pleaded for an answer. "Who were those men outside? Why were they here?"

"Your brother...he...." As she was about to set the glass onto the table, it fell the last inch from her grasp, landed with a thud, and the liquor splashed.

"Jason? He what?"

Carolyn collapsed into a chair.

"Mom! He what?"

After what seemed an eternity, she sobbed through quick breaths. "Today...in a training...accident...he...." She mustered enough strength to gather her next words and stare directly into his eyes. "Was killed." Her head dropped into her hands. "Oh, Jason, oh my dear, dear son." Tears drowned her.

Stunned, John could not move. "Jason? What? He can't be! I just talked...."

Finally, she gasped her next words, "His plane...had some...kind of...malfunction." John reached to embrace his mother. "He was the purest soul...I've ever known."

As he held her, his mind flooded with memories of meals they shared, conversation, adventures of the past, adventures that would never come. All became...numb. Mother and son held each other, unable to contain the emotion, and their cries became one.

Finally, she pushed back. "When they found the wreckage...there were no survivors."

John wiped his eyes with his sleeve, and she tried to gather herself with another drink.

"You must be strong for your sister, for Sarah, for Megan, and for...." She reached for his hand and placed it against her cheek. "And for me."

John nodded. "I will. I will. I promise."

Slowly, she released his hand. "I must go to Jennifer. She is in her room. She was asleep.... I don't know." In a daze, she staggered from the room.

Before realizing it, he found himself in the family room. Pictures hung on the wall behind him in neat perfection. Dropping onto the couch, he sat on a pile of comics. Reaching underneath, he pulled the books out. For a moment, he stared at them and managed a half-smile as he thought of his little sister. He wiped his eyes again.

Then without warning, he threw the comics across the room where they fluttered to the floor. Dropping his head into his hands, he dissolved into tears once more.

Chapter Twenty-Seven

Green Shamrocks

As the Mann family sat next to Jason's casket, the rain slowed and gradually ended. John took a deep breath of spring air and absorbed his surroundings.

An American flag draped the casket in direct view of the family. A firing party of five rifle-bearers stood poised at attention about fifty yards from the gravesite but in clear view. A single bugler positioned with the color guard about thirty yards from the grave. Despite the tragedy and the confluence of thoughts swirling in John's mind, he felt oddly at ease as he observed the ceremony.

The patriotism of the participants impressed him. He'd thought the precision and order of a military funeral would indicate a cool detachment.

On that morning, though, its effect seemed just the opposite. The truly patriotic protocol comforted. It gave direction to what otherwise seemed to be a senseless tragedy.

"Please stand for the rendering of honors," the funeral director said.

John stared at the flag that hovered over his brother's coffin. Three soldiers supported the flag on each side. Their white gloves gripped the edges of it, a firm, yet respectful, delicacy in every touch.

The sound of a military voice broke the quiet. "Firing party...attention." The rifle party moved as one and acted with precision.

She's not going to be prepared. He grabbed Jennifer's hand.

"Stand by...ready."

The party tapped their rifles to the ground and raised them to the sky in salute.

He lifted his eyes to the heavens. *The clouds...beautiful...it's starting to clear.*

"Ready."

He turned to his mother. *The pain she must.... I never realized how strong—*

"Aim."

He stared at his sister. *Everything is going to*

be fine, sis, but I—

"Fire."

John squeezed her hand as Jennifer flinched with each of the three volleys fired over the gravesite.

"Present arms!"

The lone sound of the bugler cut through the morning air. As "Taps" played, it reminded John—again—it was the saddest song he ever heard.

A stern military voice commanded, "Order arms!"

"Please be seated," the director said.

John watched the flag properly folded. Even something as seemingly simple as that had ritual.

The detail leader presented it to Sarah. "Ma'am, On behalf of the President of the United States, the United States Navy, and a grateful nation, please accept this flag as a symbol of our appreciation for your loved one's honorable and faithful service. We share in grieving over the loss of your husband."

As she accepted the flag, her composure amazed John. The detail leader hand-saluted her for three seconds and offered condolences to the remainder of the family.

Jason's commander followed and spoke to Carolyn. "Mrs. Mann, your son was the finest of a large number of fine young men I have ever commanded. I am most sorry for your loss. May God bless you and give you strength in your time of need."

As the funeral drew to a close, people filed from the site. John looked to his left. Carolyn consoled Sarah. Jennifer sat silently waiting for her brother's cue.

He approached the casket. Before the funeral, someone had placed a handful of shamrocks atop. They'd sat beneath the flag the entire service, and with the flag removed, they could be truly noticed. Their life-giving green color contrasted sharply with the cold, dark surface. The shamrock had been at the heart of Jason's squadron patch. His brother called it a zapper. John stared at each of the clover's three distinct spheres.

Jennifer moved to his side, and he collected two shamrocks. Handing one to her, he placed the other inside the left pocket of his sport coat.

Without a word, she clutched his hand and they stared in disbelief.

***

The generosity of their friends overwhelmed them. Tables displayed an array of pies, pastas, chicken, salads, and desserts upon the Mann's return. Family members mingled with various military personnel and friends who had come to support them.

Someone had already taken the flag from Sarah and encased it in a wooden display case. Surrounded by flowers, it sat next to a color picture of Jason when he'd first received his wings. The display stood at the center of the dining room table.

John glanced around the room. Carolyn talked to the priest from St. Mary's. Sarah held a quiet discussion with Megan. Jennifer asked a sergeant about the intricacies of flying. The early afternoon seemed to drag like a tired clock.

He ate little and listened a lot. Then he had an idea.

Walking over to his mother, he whispered into her ear. When she gave an approving nod, he went to a kitchen drawer and retrieved the keys to his mother's car.

Chapter Twenty-Eight

Letter of Inspiration

John entered the Old Man's room and found it empty. Before he could gather his thoughts, a nurse arrived with an armful of bed sheets.

"Oh, John. I didn't know you were here."

"Where's...? Did something happen? Is he...?"

"No, he's fine. He packed and left last night. Said he had to go somewhere important and that you would understand. She set the fresh sheets next to the bed. "Wait right here. He left something for you."

She soon returned with an envelope and a package. "He wanted you to have these." She handed them to him.

"I don't understand."

"He said you would. It was good seeing you,

John." She began to make the bed.

Taking the envelope and package, he left.

***

Numb, John sat on the park bench and tried to absorb the events of the last few days. The package the nurse had given him sat to his right, the envelope to his left. He raised his head to better view the birdhouses in the sky, took a deep breath, and turned his attention to the American flag.

He thought of the flag outstretched on Jason's coffin. It rested in a display case. Reaching into his sport coat, he took the shamrock out. He ran it through his fingers, glanced again at the multitude of birdhouses, and drew another breath.

Placing the shamrock on top of the package, he opened the envelope to reveal a handwritten letter. As he began to read, he could almost hear the Old Man's voice as if he were sitting next to him.

Dear John,

For many years now I have been in search of something I was never able to find or, more importantly, fully grasp. I have tried so hard to put the events of sixty years ago out of mind, only to have them return to haunt me, over and over. Throughout the last few months, you have made me realize what I had forgotten. Too often people try to forget the most difficult times of their lives, rather than embrace them and be reminded of the very things they need...that life is short, fragile, and not always fair. I have come to realize what happened all those years ago has made me the man I am today.

Heroes do not have to do tremendous deeds like Superman or give their cars to charity. In fact, many heroes walk through life quietly, honestly, and respectfully. Their actions are noble and selfless. But in the face of adversity, heroes endure and persevere. Heroism can be found in the smallest of acts, from people of all ages and sizes, as long as their intentions are true. When the time comes for action, it is in this decision to act, to put themselves out there for everyone to see that separates men. It is at that moment, when they are exposed for who they are and what they stand for, that makes most shrink.

You were right to remind me of my own words...without fear there can be no courage, without courage there can be no honor, and without honor there can be no heroes. I was so afraid all those years ago. But being a hero is not being fearless or telling others what is heroic. Being a hero is making a difference for the people around you and those you may never know. What we did on the Indianapolis all those years ago did make a difference.

And that is what you have done for me. You have made a difference. I am so proud of the man you have become. You will always be a hero to me.

John didn't open the package but grabbed it and stood. With the envelope and letter in one hand and the package in the other, he began to walk. Passing one of the birdhouses, he paused, placed the shamrock on it, and continued to the car.

The drive would take less than fifteen minutes.

Chapter Twenty-Nine

Unsung Heroes

John moved quickly through the halls. Summer session I had started the previous week, and everyone sat in class. Approaching the door, he stopped and glimpsed inside. Students filled the room as Dr. Shelly rambled in the middle of a lecture.

Without fear there can be no courage. He drew a deep breath, grabbed the handle, and entered the room.

Shelly's words trailed off when John approached her. "And that is...the quest...for truth...."

The classroom sat in complete silence.

"Still searching for heroes, Dr. Shelly?" John's confident air masked whatever apprehension remained. "When will you realize that true heroism occupies a sacred space most will never know, yourself included."

Muttered curses and shocked gasps of disbelief circulated throughout the room. A few students whispered, while others shook their heads as if they recognized him. Many reached for their cell phones. Shelly stood, frozen.

He stepped toward her podium and addressed the class as the instructor. "So, once again you are asked, what is a hero? The word implies bravery, extraordinary achievement, sacrifice for others and often in the face of personal danger. The Greeks tell us that heroic tradition includes elements of courage, outstanding achievement, and the overcoming of formidable obstacles."

"I have heard enough from you," Shelly began. "You need to—"

John turned on her. "And you need to listen!" Again he spoke to the class. "Heroic identity is not concerned with show or witness. A hero doesn't act for recognition or applause." He met her gaze. "Or for a grade."

Unbeknownst to him, Steve had recorded the event on his cell phone several months earlier. It was the very day John thought he knew what it meant to be a hero, the day he donated his car. He'd posted the video, a description of Shelly's offer, along with details about John's donation, and the final grade. He even included an actual picture of John's report card on a social media website. All students and administrators at Pensacola Community College had received at that moment a priority email prompting them to the website.

"What matters to heroes is whether or not they have made a difference. Put yourself to the hazard, Dr. Shelly. Honor? Courage? Truth? You throw around words like an angry child throws around toys."

"I'm calling security." She moved to a phone hanging on the wall.

The students' attention bounced between her and John. Apparently, the tennis match had resumed, and he hammered away.

"As you sit in the safety of this room, surrounded by these walls, protected by the real heroes of our world, all you do is preach to others about the universal struggle of life and death. Remember the real heroes are quite simply the ones who try to make a difference, and their only intentions are to help those who can't do it for themselves. Their motives are pure, and the only truth they know, or need to, is what they ought to do...and they do it."

Shelly hung up the phone, helpless as he moved for the exit, his gaze fixed on his former professor. "There is a difference between wisdom and knowledge, and you would be wise to know this." He grabbed the door handle and paused. "You did get one thing right. You once said, 'In the end, heroes will lead and others will follow.'"

Dumbfounded, she didn't respond. Many of the students finished watching the video and reading Steve's post. Expressions of disgust shot from student to professor. As John walked through the door, a girl in the front row rose and exited the room behind him. Another followed, and then another. One by one, they paraded out the door after him.

"Where are you going?" Shelly demanded. "I didn't tell you to leave! You are not allowed to go! Get back here!"

But students continued to file out of the room.

"I said come back! *Come back here! Now!*"

Through the hall, John disappeared into a sea

of students.

***

The birdhouse park seemed unusually busy. Birds darted everywhere as the sun bathed the scene in idyllic light.

Almost the golden hour.

He reminisced how as boys Jason had first told him about it. They'd been hiking with their father out West. As they reached the summit of a very large hill, Jason paused. He'd peered back at his little brother and pointed to the setting sun. "It's called the golden hour because for a brief window of time, the light of day is like no other."

Roy had heard their conversation. "If you think it's something to see on the ground, you should see it from the air. It's as if everything is right with the world and all your troubles are forgotten."

Jason had told John that night it was then, after hearing father, he wanted to be a pilot.

John sat by himself in the middle of the park. A small bird landed next to him, almost within arm's length. It tilted its head and stared. He smiled at the bird's brazenness. And just as quickly, it flew away, upward, past the flag waving lazily above. He thought about the view his father and Jason must have.

"Your mom told me you might be here." Startled, he spun to see Steve approaching.

John pointed at the surrounding birdhouses. "So, what do you think?"

"Unbelievable." Steve sat next to him and smiled. "He made every one of these?"

"Yeah, every one. By the way, I just got a text from Megan."

"Really?"

"She told me what you did, about the video you made and what you wrote on the website. I can't believe you posted the entire thing for the school to see."

"They needed to see for themselves what you did, what you sacrificed. Shelly will get what she deserves." Steve's smile began to widen. "Don't worry about it...anything for a friend."

"Well, I want to thank you. It means a lot to me." John turned and faced him. "It made a difference." John's tone became accusatory but playful. "And somehow all the students seemed to know about it at the same time, and right in the middle of her class!"

"Really?" Steve smirked.

"Yeah, I wonder how that happened?"

"You got me? But campus priority email must be an amazing thing."

Steve stared at the ground, a sheepish grin spread from ear to ear. "Anyway, anything for a friend. I heard the whole class walked out on her."

"I don't know about that. I didn't really stick around. She called security."

"Good thing. We both know how good you are with cops." Steve spun toward him. "And besides, they were probably armed with a fistful of pens."

The best friends burst into laughter as they sat and absorbed their surroundings.

A sense of seriousness crept into Steve's tone. "You know, your brother would be proud of you."

"You think?"

"What you did? I could never do. That took guts. I mean, you put it all out there for everyone to see."

"Actually, you did that."

For a moment, both sat still and focused on the birds flying around the park.

"Is it just me, or are there are a lot of birds

around here?"

"Sailors that made it home," John muttered.

"What?"

"Remind me to tell you about it later."

John stood and approached the nearest birdhouse. He leaned against the post and watched the birds soaring above. "The only thing is that I never...I never got a chance to say good-bye to Jason, to tell him what he meant to me, to our family."

"Well, what's stopping you?"

"What's stopping me from what?"

"I said what's stopping you from saying good-bye?"

Suddenly, John had a spark in his eye as if he just remembered something, and started to jog quickly away. "I'll talk to you later."

"Where you going?"

John slipped into a sprint and yelled back. "I'm taking your advice."

"Advice?" Steve asked. "What advice?"

John continued to run.

"What advice?" Steve's shoulders slumped. "And just so you know, I don't have a ride home! I guess I'll just have to...." He scratched his head, took a deep sigh, and mumbled, "Take the bus...again."

John vanished into the trees. And though it was quite faint, his friend's final words reached him. "Maybe I'll just get a bowl of red beans and rice while I am at it!"

***

When John returned home, the guests had left. Carolyn, Megan, Sarah, and Jennifer were taking down folding chairs and straightening the house.

His sense of strength renewed, he went to his mother. "Mom, I think there's one last thing we have to do." Addressing the others in the room, he added, "Come on. I want to take you somewhere."

The family followed him out the door and into the car.

***

When the family arrived, the setting sun lit up the cemetery with a molten-golden glow. As they made their way to Jason's gravesite, John carried the package from the Old Man. They gathered around the grave, much like they did at prayer before dinner. The smell of fresh dirt hung in the air.

"When Jason flew, he used to say, 'Heaven above, earth below, and I am somewhere in between.'" John raised his eyes to the skies and smiled. "I like to think that when he flew, he was with angels, and now, in his final journey, they've carried him back to touch the face of God. It was never a question of having to prove something. For Jason, and the unsung heroes that walk among us, we may never know when or how, but their actions echo for eternity. May they rest in peace."

Carolyn put her arms around her son and held him close. "That was beautiful, John."

His attention fell to the package he still held.

"Who's that from?" Jennifer asked.

"A very good friend of mine." He opened it as everyone watched.

Jennifer inquired again. "Who?"

He paused for a moment. "You should know, Jen. It's from a hero, a real-life hero." He reached inside and thought of Jason's words the previous Christmas when John had taken his brother to meet the Old Man and given him the sextant.

This ought to be interesting.

He cleared the very old newspaper to reveal something familiar. Something the Old Man and John had first built together.

"It's a birdhouse!" Jennifer squealed.

John broke into a smile.

"What? What're you smiling about?" Megan said.

His voice hushed, John addressed them. "The Old Man once told me birdhouses were a gift...a gift that helps every lost sailor find his way home."

He reached into the box again. "And there's something else." He pulled the Old Man's framed medal from the box.

"What is it?" Jennifer asked.

"It's his medal, from the *Indianapolis*." He handed it to his mother, who in turn shared it with her.

For an instant, the Mann family was one again. And as they held each other in the final moments of the setting sun, John's burden lifted.

And as he stood there, he began to hear it. Imperceptible at first, the faint sound continued to fill his unbelieving ears and seemed to descend from the heavens above. Seven musical notes repeated over and over. The notes seemed familiar, but he couldn't place the melody.

He shook his head to clear his mind. And just when he felt he could identify the sound, his mother spoke.

"Let's go home."

They began to walk away, but, after a few steps, Jennifer ran back to the gravesite.

Gently, she placed her favorite Superman comic next to the mound of fresh dirt.

Chapter Thirty

Fifteen Months Later
Possibilities

"How do I look?"

"Fine." Megan brushed a piece of lint off of his jacket with one hand while balancing presents in the other. An engagement ring flashed on her finger. "Now, quit fidgeting."

John held an armful of wrapped presents and knocked again on the door. This time he heard Jennifer's voice on the other side. "What's the secret password?"

He grinned at Megan and back to the closed door. "The secret pass.... You've got to be kidding me. C'mon, Jen!"

"*What* is the secret password?" replied the voice within, a bit louder than before.

Megan shrugged. Finally, he responded, "Fortress of Solitude!"

The door remained closed.

Megan shifted the presents in her arms. "Happy Birthday?"

The door burst open, and Jennifer ran through the entrance and embraced them both. Grabbing Megan by the hand, she led her into the house. Birthday decorations were everywhere and a giant banner hung above the hearth displaying its message in proud boldness, *Happy 1st Birthday J.J.!*

J.J. sat on the floor, a little wobbly, but happy and content. Jennifer joined her nephew and danced a toy figurine of the Incredible Hulk around the baby.

As John searched the room, he eyed his mother. The Old Man sat by her side. John moved to join them.

Carolyn hugged her son and whispered, "I'll give you two a moment." She disappeared into the kitchen.

He sat next to the Old Man and leaned toward him. "My mom told me you would be here."

"Did she?"

"She did." John placed his hand on his shoulder and gave it a tender squeeze. "It is good to see you again, friend."

The Old Man growled softly and smiled. "And you, too, son. When I left, I went to the reunion in Indianapolis, the one you told me about. It was time to go back and just felt right. After it was over, I was invited to stay with one of my closest friends on the ship, the one I told you about who lost his pants when the ship went down." His smile faded. "He died about a month ago. I decided to return to Saint Francis' shortly after."

"I'm sorry."

"I appreciate that but, you know, the same end awaits us all. We can't choose *when*, but we can choose *how* to live our lives and *how* to be remembered. That's what matters." He watched J.J. and Jennifer playing on the floor and chuckled.

Jennifer walked to him and pointed to his forearm. "What's your tattoo of?" He lifted his sleeve to reveal an anchor held by a hawk. "An eagle!"

"No, Jennifer, it's a hawk."

"What does it mean?"

"Many sailors get this when they join the Navy.

It's kind of a symbol, like making a pledge."

"Kinda like the S on Superman's chest?"

"Exactly. Kinda like the S on Superman's chest." The Old Man glanced at John and smiled again. "The tattoo is a promise that sailors make to themselves and each other, to be brave and willing to sacrifice."

"Neat!" She spun and returned to J.J.'s side.

The Old Man's face became serious, and he motioned to John to come nearer. "I read about your brother's death shortly after I left. He truly was a hero."

"Just like you."

He grasped John's neck. "You know, a funny thing happened over the past year."

"What's that?"

"Ever since that reunion in Indianapolis, I haven't had any more nightmares. I think I'm finally at peace with myself and what happened all those years ago." He continued to watch J.J. at play.

"What do you dream of now?"

The Old Man tilted his head toward John and with a child-like grin, exclaimed, "Possibilities."

Sarah picked her son up and placed him in a high chair at the dining room table. J.J. cooed his approval.

"Everyone gather around!" Carolyn walked around the corner holding a birthday cake, complete with lit candles.

The family came together much like prayer at dinner and began to sing.

When the birthday song ended, Jennifer's voice rose above the rest. "Look, Mommy, Jason Jr.'s eyes!"

"What about them, honey?"

"They're the color of the ocean!"

"Yes, dear...yes, they are. Just like your father's."

Chapter Thirty-One

The Golden Hour

The setting sun cast an idyllic light onto the Mann house. One wall in particular was struck by the golden glow—the wall covered with pictures of Roy, and Jason, and family. The photographs hung neatly, and in one panoramic view a lifetime of memories swept past.

Tucked into the center of the display were two newly added, framed medals.

They hung conspicuously next to Roy's.

Once again, love, laughter, and celebration filled the Mann household.

***

And then, it began.

If one listened closely, a sound began to emanate. It was not the sound of man, or ocean, or beast.

Instead, it was quiet, and soft, and peaceful, like the steady rain of a passing storm.

As John absorbed the familial scene before him, his brother's words rang in his ears.

Heaven above, Earth below....

He walked to the window, and the dazzling light of the golden hour illuminated him. Staring outside, he searched the landscape.

Again the sound came.

And as he continued to stare, a complete sense of satisfaction washed through him. He no longer had to search. Everything he wanted, everything he needed, was in that room.

The Old Man's laugh caught his attention and he turned back to his family.

But the sound pulled his gaze to the window one final time.

Heaven above, Earth below....

John leaned his head against the cool glass pane and softly finished his brother's thought.

"And I am somewhere in between."

Beyond the smiling faces and sunlit room, down the hall and just outside the house, perched a small bird. Bathed in golden light, it sat on a golden birdhouse, singing its golden song.

As laughter echoed inside the house, the bird's sweet sound rang out. Seven familiar notes, over and over...a church song he'd learned as a boy...many years ago.

Final Thoughts

When I received word Jason had died in a low-level training accident in 2006, I was blind-sided. I could only imagine the devastation his parents and loved ones felt. His story would stay with me, much like the "melody" stuck with Jason throughout the entire story.

Above all, my intention is to honor Jason's memory and all veterans who make the ultimate sacrifice. When he died, he left behind a wife and an unborn son, Griffith, who is now nine years old.

It should be noted a portion of all net proceeds gathered from the sale of this story will be donated to the Lt. Jason Manse Memorial Fund that will support a scholarship at Central Catholic High School in Canton, Ohio. The scholarship will be awarded to a deserving senior who is entering the military.

I encourage everyone to visit my website HeavenAboveEarthBelow.com. One can find more information as to how this story was constructed...kind of like the bonus material on a DVD. In addition to seeing pictures of the actual items that provided inspiration, the song "Heaven

Above, Earth Below" can be heard. Sung by my daughter Angela, it was first performed at a Father's Day Mass last year.

Mark Perretta

March 22, 2016

About the Author

Mark was born on Thanksgiving Day in 1967 and raised in a very loving family. His mother taught grade school and father worked as a school psychologist. As he and his sister grew up, they quickly became used to summer vacations in Nags Head, N.C. Ironically, it was much later in life that a vacation to the same Outer Banks would serve as the final inspiration needed to write *Heaven Above, Earth Below*.

After attending St. Thomas Aquinas High School in Louisville, Ohio, Mark earned his B.A. in Communications, Journalism, English and his certification as a teacher from John Carroll and Walsh Universities. He dabbled in television broadcasting, but would eventually enter the world of education. His first job came at Canton Central Catholic High School where he worked as a Theology teacher. He taught at Central for three years and coached football, track and speech. While at Central, he would meet the real-life Jason who would become the driving force behind his story.

In 1994 he would marry and be blessed over the next few years with three children. After three years at Central Catholic, he taught at Canton McKinley High School for seven years, teaching mostly British Literature and Journalism. Canton South High School provides his current workplace where he currently teaches American Literature and Journalism, and is finishing his 24th year of teaching.

Mark's debut novella, *Heaven Above, Earth Below* is a heart-warming tale that twists together the lives of three men. It magically celebrates family, faith, honor, and sacrifice.